Atlas Drummond: Fragments of Deceit

A Thriller

by

Jackie L. Smith

Copyright Page

Copyright © 2026 by Jackie L. Smith

Published by Jackie L. Smith

Cover design by Jessica Stacey

ISBN: 979-8-9959280-5-8 (paperback)

Printed and Published in the United States of America

Dedication

For the men and women who serve in silence,

who sacrifice in shadows,

and who fight for justice when no one is watching.

And for my family,

who endured countless deployments and late nights

with grace, patience, and unwavering support.

Chapter 1: A Night Out

The text message came through at 9:47 PM.

"Atlas, your father's in trouble. Call me. NOW."

Atlas Drummond stared at his phone, his mother's message glowing in the dim light of his apartment. He'd ignored three calls from her already tonight. Now this.

He should call back. He knew he should.

Instead, he pocketed his phone, grabbed his leather jacket, and headed out into the rain.

The guilt would be there whether he called now or in an hour. Might as well have a drink first.

The rain came down in sheets, turning the downtown streets into a mosaic of reflected neon and streetlight. Atlas stood under the flickering awning of McGinty's Bar, watching the storm and contemplating whether going inside was really better than going home to his empty apartment.

At 38, he'd spent enough nights in places like this

to know exactly what waited—stale beer, forced laughter, people trying to forget their problems. But the alternative was four walls and silence.

And his mother's message burning in his pocket.

Your father's in trouble.

When wasn't the old man in trouble? Probably his computer acting up again. Or the car making that noise. Or some conspiracy theory he'd fallen down the rabbit hole on.

Atlas ran a hand through his short, dark hair, feeling the rain that had already soaked through during his walk from the parking garage. Six years in the Army, including two tours overseas. Now he worked day shift security for a downtown corporate complex—checking employee IDs at the front desk, reviewing surveillance footage, writing incident reports about stolen keyboards and parking disputes, pretending his life had purpose.

With a resigned sigh, he pushed through the heavy wooden door.

The wall of sound hit him first. Classic rock from the jukebox, overlapping conversations, the sharp crack of pool balls. McGinty's was packed for a Thursday night, bodies pressed together at the bar, every booth occupied.

Atlas made his way through the crowd, his size and bearing causing people to step aside. At six-foot-two and two hundred pounds of mostly muscle, he had a presence. His blue eyes swept the room in a habitual scan—exits, threats, troublemakers. Old habits from the military died hard.

"Atlas!" The bartender, Lola, spotted him and smiled. Bottle-blonde, mid-fifties, face that had seen everything. "Haven't seen you in a couple weeks. Thought maybe you'd found a classier joint."

"You know me, Lola. I'm not a classy guy." He settled onto his usual stool at the end of the bar. "The usual?"

"Double Jameson, neat. Coming right up." She poured with practiced efficiency. "You look like you need it tonight. Rough day?"

"Rough week." He accepted the glass, let the whiskey burn down his throat. "Got the kids this weekend though."

"That's good." Lola wiped down the bar. "Your folks doing okay?"

Atlas thought about the text message. Your father's in trouble.

"Yeah," he lied. "They're fine."

The whiskey was going down smooth, warming him from the inside. The ambient noise was almost comforting—a cocoon where nobody expected anything from him. Not Atlas the son, not Atlas the father, not Atlas the disappointment. Just a guy having a drink.

He was contemplating ordering a second when she walked in.

The door opened, bringing rain-scented air and a woman who made Atlas forget how to breathe.

She was tall—maybe five-nine—with a cascade of red hair that fell past her shoulders in natural waves, darker where it was wet. Jeans that fit perfectly, knee-high boots, black leather jacket. But it was her face that caught him. Strong features, high cheekbones, and eyes that were scanning the room with the same careful assessment he'd just done.

Green eyes. Striking, intelligent green eyes.

Their gazes locked for just a second, and Atlas felt something he hadn't experienced in years— genuine interest. Not just attraction.

Actual curiosity about who this person was.

She made her way to the bar, moving with confidence. When a drunk guy stumbled into her path, she sidestepped without breaking stride, and there was something in the efficiency of that movement that suggested training.

"What can I get you?" Lola asked.

"Maker's Mark, rocks." Her voice was lower than Atlas expected. Husky and warm with a slight accent he couldn't place.

She scanned the crowded bar for a seat. After a moment, her eyes came back to Atlas and the empty stool next to him.

Atlas saw her weighing her options. He gave her a small nod, tried to make his expression non-threatening, and gestured to the stool. "It's all yours if you want it. I don't bite."

She studied him for another moment, those green eyes taking his measure. Then something in her expression relaxed fractionally. "Thanks."

She claimed the stool, shrugging out of her wet jacket. Underneath she wore a simple black V-neck sweater. Atlas tried not to stare.

"Rough night to be out," he said.

"Rough night to be anywhere." She took a sip of her bourbon. "At least it's warm and dry in here."

"That's about all McGinty's has going for it, but it's enough."

She smiled—a quick flash that transformed her face. "You a regular?"

"More regular than I probably should be. You?"

"First time. I'm new to the area." She extended her hand. "Hollis. Hollis Brooks."

Atlas shook her hand, noting the firm grip and small scars on her knuckles. Hands that had seen work. "Atlas Drummond. Most people call me Ace."

"Ace? That's got to have a story."

"Nothing exciting. Army nickname that stuck."
The real story involved a hostage rescue in
Kandahar, but that didn't play well in bars. "I was
decent at cards."

"Army," Hollis said, understanding in her tone.
"How long?"

"Six years. Got out four years ago. You?"

She shook her head. "Not military. But my dad
was. Marines."

"Jarhead, huh? Well, nobody's perfect." He
smiled to show he was joking.

Hollis laughed, genuine and warm. "He'd have
said the same thing about Army guys. God rest him."

"Sorry for your loss."

"Thanks. It was a while ago." She didn't
elaborate, and Atlas didn't push.

His phone buzzed in his pocket. He ignored it.

They sat in comfortable silence for a few
minutes, both nursing their drinks. Springsteen's
"Thunder Road" played on the jukebox.

"So what brings you to our fair city?" Atlas asked. "Work?"

"Consulting. IT security. Companies hire me to test their systems, find vulnerabilities." Hollis swirled her ice. "It's steady work. Lets me move around."

"You like moving around?"

"Haven't found a good reason to stay put yet." She turned to face him more directly. "What about you? What do you do when you're not being Ace?"

"Corporate security. Office building downtown. Checking IDs, reviewing surveillance footage, making sure nobody's stealing computers." He shrugged. "Mostly boring, but it lets me have a regular schedule. Means I get to see my kids regularly. That's what matters."

"Kids?" Hollis's eyebrows raised. "You're married?"

"Divorced. Three years now. Amicable, mostly." He searched for words. "We wanted different things. Or maybe I wasn't capable of being what she needed. Either way, it ended. But we've got two great kids. Emma's nine, Josh is seven."

"That's good. That you stayed on good terms."

"We try." Atlas finished his whiskey and signaled Lola. "Can I get you a refill?"

Hollis glanced at her nearly empty glass, seemed to weigh something. Then she nodded. "Sure. Why not?"

His phone buzzed again. He silenced it without looking.

They fell into easier conversation. Atlas learned that Hollis had grown up in Atlanta, moved around for college and work, had a complicated relationship with commitment. She'd been engaged once but it hadn't worked out. She liked classic rock, preferred bourbon to vodka, had a sarcastic sense of humor he appreciated.

Atlas found himself telling her things he didn't usually share—about adjusting after the Army, trying to be a good father while battling his own demons, his complicated relationship with his parents.

"So your dad's pretty demanding, huh?" Hollis asked.

"Old school. Doesn't understand why I can't drop everything the second he needs something." Atlas rotated his glass. "I love him, but he drives me crazy."

"Sounds familiar. My dad was like that too." Hollis's expression went distant. "I miss him anyway. Miss that connection, even when it was frustrating."

"Yeah. I suppose I'll miss the old man when he's gone too."

They drank to that.

Atlas's phone buzzed a third time. He pulled it out, ready to silence it again, when he saw the preview of his mother's latest message:

"Atlas, please. Your father found something. People are following him. He's scared. Call me."

The warmth drained from his body.

"Everything okay?" Hollis asked, noticing the change in his expression.

"I... I don't know." Atlas stood up, suddenly sober despite the whiskey. "I need to make a call. I'm sorry."

"No, go. Do what you need to do."

Atlas stepped outside into the rain, dialing his mother's number. It rang once.

Then went straight to voicemail.

He tried his father's phone. Same thing.

People are following him. He's scared.

His father didn't scare easily. Thomas Drummond was a lot of things—stubborn, opinionated, frustrating—but he wasn't the type to panic.

Atlas was dialing 911 when he noticed the black SUV parked across the street. Engine running. Headlights off. Someone sitting in the driver's seat, watching him.

His military training kicked in hard. Every sense went on high alert.

The SUV's door opened.

Atlas's hand moved instinctively to his waistband, where his concealed carry weapon rested. The figure approaching from the SUV was big, moving with professional purpose. Dark clothes, careful scan of surroundings.

"Atlas Drummond?" The voice was deep, professional.

"Who's asking?"

"Someone who needs to have a conversation with you. About your father."

Ice formed in Atlas's stomach. "What about my father?"

"He's been looking into things he shouldn't. Asking questions. Collecting information." The man took a step closer. "That needs to stop."

"I don't know what you're talking about."

"Yes, you do. Or you will soon enough." The man's expression didn't change. "Your father has been investigating something called Project Genesis. He's gathered evidence about things that should stay buried. We need that evidence, Mr. Drummond. All of it."

Atlas's mind raced. Project Genesis? He'd never

heard of it.

"And if I don't have it?"

The man pulled out his phone, showed Atlas a video feed. His parents' house. His mother visible through the window, moving around the kitchen. Alone. Vulnerable.

"Then we'll have to have a conversation with your mother instead. She's home right now, as you can see. We have people very close to her. One word from me..."

Atlas's hands clenched into hard fists. "If you hurt her—"

"That depends entirely on your cooperation." The man pulled out a business card, set it on the hood of Atlas's truck. "You have forty-eight hours to find everything your father collected about Project Genesis and prepare to hand it over. If you cooperate, your parents go free. If you don't..."

He let the sentence hang.

"I want proof they're alive."

"You'll get it. When you call that number." The man gestured to the card. "Forty-eight hours, Mr.

Drummond. And don't involve the police. We'll know if you do."

He turned and walked back to the SUV, got in, and drove away.

Atlas stood in the rain, hands shaking, the business card in his hand. Plain white, no name or company. Just a phone number.

Behind him, the door to McGinty's opened. Hollis stepped out.

"Atlas? What's going on? You look like you've seen a ghost."

He turned to face her, and she must have seen something in his expression because her whole demeanor changed. Went alert, ready.

"Someone just threatened my parents," Atlas said, his voice flat. "Said my father's been investigating something called Project Genesis. That they'll kill him if I don't hand over evidence I don't even know exists."

"Project Genesis?" Something flickered in Hollis's eyes. Recognition. "Atlas, what did your father do for a living?"

"Insurance adjuster. Why?"

Hollis's face had gone pale. "My father died of a heart attack five years ago. The insurance investigator on his case was named Thomas Drummond."

They stared at each other in the rain, the connection forming between them. Not chance. Not coincidence.

"I think," Hollis said slowly, "we need to talk. Somewhere private. Right now."

Atlas's phone buzzed. A text from the unknown number:

"Tick tock, Mr. Drummond. 47 hours, 58 minutes remaining. Your mother is making tea. She has no idea we're watching. Let's keep it that way."

Attached was a photo. His mother in her Kitchen. Taken from outside the window. Taken moments ago.

"We need to go," Atlas said. "Now."

Whatever this was, whatever his father had stumbled into, it was bigger and more dangerous than Atlas had imagined.

And the clock was already ticking.

Chapter 2: Connections

They drove to Atlas's apartment in tense silence, Hollis following in her rental car. Atlas kept checking his mirrors, looking for the black SUV or any other tail. The streets were empty, rain-slicked and gleaming under streetlights, but that didn't mean they weren't being watched.

His mind raced through the implications. His father, investigating something called Project Genesis. Hollis's father, dead five years ago, his case handled by Thomas Drummond. The man in the parking lot, the threats, the countdown.

Forty-seven hours and change.

Atlas pulled into the underground parking garage of his apartment building, waited for Hollis to park beside him. They took the elevator up in silence, both hyper-aware of the security camera in the corner. Atlas wondered if someone was watching that feed right now. If they already knew he'd brought Hollis here.

His apartment was on the fourth floor—a small one-bedroom that felt more like a way station than a home. Functional furniture, no pictures on the walls except a few photos of Emma and Josh. A place to sleep

between workdays and weekends that actually mattered.

Atlas locked the door behind them, checked the windows, drew the curtains. Old habits.

"You think they're watching us?" Hollis asked, standing in the middle of his living room.

"I think they've been watching me since this started. Maybe before." Atlas pulled out the business card, set it on the coffee table like it might explode. "And I think we need to figure out what the hell Project Genesis is before that clock runs out."

Hollis pulled out her laptop from her bag—she'd grabbed it from her car before coming up. "Tell me everything you know about your father's work. Everything."

Atlas paced while he talked, unable to sit still. "Thomas Drummond, sixty-eight years old. Worked as an insurance adjuster for thirty-five years before he retired three years ago. Handled life insurance claims, investigated suspicious deaths to determine if the insurance company should pay out."

"So he was good at finding inconsistencies. At spotting when things didn't add up."

"The best. He was meticulous, obsessive even. Drove my mother crazy with how he'd bring work home, spend hours going over files." Atlas stopped pacing. "He took early retirement because the company was pushing him out. Said he was too slow, too thorough, holding up claims processing."

"Or maybe he was finding things they didn't want found," Hollis suggested, her fingers already flying over her keyboard.

"After he retired, he got bored. Started doing freelance consulting for smaller insurance companies, helping them investigate suspicious claims." Atlas ran his hand through his hair. "He'd call me sometimes, complain about cases that didn't sit right with him. Deaths that were ruled natural but seemed suspicious. Medical records that didn't match up."

"Did he ever mention Project Genesis?"

"Never. Not once." Atlas pulled out his phone, looked at his mother's text messages again. Your father found something. People are following him. "But these past few weeks, he's been different. Distracted. He'd call and ask weird questions—how to encrypt files, how to use a VPN, whether I still had contacts in the military."

"You think he knew he was onto something dangerous."

"I think he knew exactly what he was onto." Atlas's jaw tightened. "And I ignored the signs. Thought he was just being paranoid, going down another conspiracy rabbit hole."

Hollis looked up from her screen. "Don't. Whatever this is, you couldn't have known. And beating yourself up won't help us find him."

She was right, but the guilt still sat heavy in Atlas's chest. How many calls had he ignored? How many times had his father reached out and Atlas had been too busy, too tired, too annoyed to really listen?

"Tell me about your father," Atlas said, needing to shift focus. "Robert Brooks. What do you remember about his death?"

Hollis's expression tightened. "Dad was fifty-two. Retired Marine, twenty years of service. He was healthy—ran five miles every morning, didn't smoke, barely drank. Then one day he collapsed at home. Heart attack. He was dead before the ambulance arrived."

"And my father investigated the insurance claim?"

"I never met him, but yes. Your father was the adjuster assigned to the case. The insurance company initially denied the claim, said there were irregularities in Dad's medical records. Your father spent three months investigating, and eventually the claim was approved." Hollis's fingers paused on the keyboard. "I remember being grateful. We needed that money. Mom was a mess, I was in college, and we had Dad's medical bills even though he died."

"But now you're wondering if there was more to it."

"Now I'm wondering if my father's death wasn't natural at all." Hollis pulled up a search screen. "Project Genesis. Let's see what we can find."

She typed, searched, clicked through pages. Atlas watched over her shoulder as she navigated through search results, following digital breadcrumbs with practiced efficiency.

"Nothing obvious," she muttered. "No company by that name, no public research projects, no news stories. Either it's deeply classified or it's completely illegal."

"Or both."

"Or both." Hollis switched tactics, pulling up a different screen. "Let me try something else. Dark web searches, encrypted forums, places where whistleblowers and investigators share information."

Atlas's phone rang, making them both jump. Unknown number. The same one that had texted him.

His hand was steady as he answered, putting it on speaker. "Hello."

"Mr. Drummond." The voice was different from the man in the parking lot—older, more cultured, with a slight accent Atlas couldn't place. "I trust you've discovered your parents' absence by now."

Atlas felt ice in his veins. "Where are they?"

"Safe. For the moment. Whether they remain safe depends entirely on your cooperation."

"I want proof. Let me talk to them."

A pause, then his mother's voice, shaky and scared. "Atlas? Atlas, don't give them anything. Don't—"

The phone was yanked away. "As you can hear, your mother is alive and unharmed. Your father is as well, though he's being somewhat less cooperative than your mother."

"If you hurt them—"

"We won't. Not if you do exactly as we say." The voice turned businesslike. "Your father has been investigating Project Genesis for six months. He's collected documents, made copies, spoken to people he shouldn't have spoken to. We need everything he's gathered. Every file, every piece of evidence.

You have forty-six hours and thirty-seven minutes remaining."

"I don't even know what Project Genesis is!"

"Then I suggest you figure it out quickly. Your father kept files, both digital and physical. Find them. Bring them to us." A pause. "And Mr. Drummond? Don't involve law enforcement. We have people everywhere. The moment we suspect you've contacted the police, your parents die. Do you understand?"

"How do I know you'll let them go even if I give you what you want?"

"You don't. But you know for certain they'll die if you don't cooperate. The choice seems clear to me."

The line went dead.

Atlas stood frozen, phone still in his hand. His mother's voice echoed in his head. Don't give them anything.

"We need to go to your father's house," Hollis said, already closing her laptop. "If he kept files, that's where they'll be."

"They might be watching the house."

"Probably. But we don't have a choice. That clock is ticking, and we need to know what we're dealing with."

Atlas grabbed his truck keys, then paused. "Hollis, you don't have to do this. This isn't your fight. You could walk away right now, go back to your hotel, and forget you ever met me."

Hollis looked at him steadily. "If Project Genesis had something to do with my father's death —if he was murdered and it was covered up as natural causes—then this absolutely is my fight." She slung her laptop bag over her shoulder. "Besides, you need someone who can handle the digital side of this. Your father was smart enough to encrypt his files, and I'm betting you're not a hacker."

"Not even close."

"Then you need me. So let's go."

The drive to his parents' house took twenty minutes. Atlas's childhood home was in a quiet suburban neighborhood, the kind of place where people knew their neighbors and crime was almost nonexistent. The kind of place that felt safe.

Both his parents' vehicles were in the driveway—his mother's Camry and his father's ancient Ford pickup. The house looked normal, peaceful even. Lights off, curtains drawn. Nothing to suggest the occupants had been kidnapped.

Atlas parked a block away, studying the house through the rain-streaked windshield. "I don't see any obvious surveillance, but that doesn't mean it's not there."

"How do you want to play this?"

"Fast and quiet. We go in through the back door—I have a key. We find whatever my father left behind, and we get out. Ten minutes, maximum."

They approached from the neighbor's yard, using the cover of trees and darkness. Atlas's military training came flooding back—how to move quietly, how to use shadows, how to make yourself small. Hollis moved with similar competence, staying low, making no unnecessary noise.

The back door was locked. Atlas let them in, his heart pounding. The house was silent, dark, and cold—the heat had been turned down, like his parents had left in a hurry.

Or been taken.

"Where would he keep important files?" Hollis whispered.

"His study. This way."

They moved through the familiar rooms of Atlas's childhood home. The Kitchen where his mother had made thousands of meals. The living room where he'd watched TV with his father, arguing about football games and politics. The hallway lined with family photos—Atlas's high school graduation, his Army promotion ceremony, Emma and Josh's baby pictures.

All of it normal. All of it a lie, because his parents weren't here and might never be here again.

His father's study was at the back of the house, a small room crammed with filing cabinets, bookshelves, and a desk buried under papers. Thomas Drummond had always been a packrat, keeping every document, every receipt, every piece of information that might be useful someday.

"Jesus," Hollis breathed, looking at the chaos. "This could take hours to sort through."

But Atlas had spotted something. The computer on the desk was gone—not just turned off, but completely removed. The cables were still there, dangling uselessly, but the tower itself had been taken.

"They already searched this place," Atlas said, his voice tight. "They took his computer."

"Then we look for what they missed." Hollis started opening filing cabinets, scanning labels. "Your father was an insurance investigator. He knew how to hide things, how to keep backup copies."

They searched systematically, quickly but thoroughly. Atlas took the desk drawers while Hollis worked through the filing cabinets. Papers everywhere—old tax returns, insurance policies, medical records, case files from his father's career.

Nothing about Project Genesis.

Atlas was about to give up when he found it— hidden in the back of the bottom desk drawer, behind a stack of old tax returns. A small key with a tag that read "SecureStore 247."

"Storage unit," Atlas said, holding up the key. "My father has a storage unit I didn't know about."

"SecureStore—isn't that the place on Industrial Boulevard?"

"Yeah." Atlas pocketed the key. "That's where he'd hide anything really important. Away from the house, in a secure location."

A sound from the front of the house made them both freeze. The front door opening. Footsteps.

"...checking the residence now," a voice said. Male, professional. "No sign of forced entry, but we'll do a full sweep."

More footsteps. Multiple people. Atlas and Hollis looked at each other, the same thought passing between them: they'd been made.

Atlas pointed to the window. Hollis nodded. They moved quickly and silently, Atlas opening the window while Hollis gathered her laptop. The voices were getting closer, coming down the hallway.

"Study's back here. That's where Drummond kept his files."

They went through the window just as the study door opened, dropping into the bushes outside. Atlas pulled the window mostly closed behind them, leaving just enough gap that it wouldn't look obviously opened.

They crawled through the wet bushes, soaking themselves, until they reached the fence separating his parents' yard from the neighbor's. Atlas boosted Hollis over, then vaulted it himself, and they ran in a low crouch back toward his truck.

Voices shouted behind them. "There! Two people heading west!"

"Go, go!" Atlas shouted, and they sprinted the last fifty yards to his truck.

He had the engine started before Hollis had her door closed, tires squealing as he pulled away from the curb. In his rearview mirror, he saw two men running out from the side of his parents' house, one pulling out a phone.

"They're calling it in," Hollis said, breathing hard. "We've got maybe five minutes before they have our location."

"Then we don't have time to be careful." Atlas took a corner too fast, the truck fishtailing slightly. "We go straight to SecureStore, grab whatever my father left there, and then we figure out our next move."

"And if they're waiting for us there?"

"Then we improvise."

They drove through the rain-soaked streets, both watching for pursuit. Atlas took a deliberately circuitous route, doubling back, taking random turns, anything to make sure they weren't being followed.

"Tell me something," Hollis said as they drove. "If your father was investigating something this dangerous for six months, why didn't he go to the police? Why keep it secret?"

"Because he was thorough. Dad wouldn't make accusations without absolute proof." Atlas ran a red light, checking his mirrors. "And maybe because he didn't know who he could trust. If these people have someone inside law enforcement, going to the cops might have just gotten him killed faster."

"They said they have people everywhere. You think that's true?"

"I think we have to assume it is. Which means we're on our own." Atlas glanced at her. "Last chance to walk away, Hollis. This is only going to get more dangerous."

"I'm not walking away." Her voice was firm. "My father might have been murdered. Your parents are being held hostage. We're in this together now."

SecureStore was a sprawling complex of orange metal buildings on the industrial side of town. Atlas pulled up to the entrance gate and used the key's RFID chip to open it. They drove through rows of identical storage units until they found building C.

Unit 247 was on the third floor. They took the stairs quickly, both scanning for any sign they'd been followed or that someone was waiting for them.

The unit was clear. Atlas unlocked it and pulled up the rolling door to reveal a ten-by-ten space filled with boxes, old furniture, and stacks of paperwork.

"There's so much," Hollis said, looking at the accumulated evidence of decades.

But Atlas had spotted it immediately—a small fireproof safe sitting on a shelf near the back, the kind used to protect important documents. And unlike everything else in the cluttered unit, it looked new.

He pulled it down. It had an electronic keypad lock. Taped to the top was a small piece of paper with two words in his father's handwriting: 'Your legacy.' Atlas's throat tightened. His legacy—Emma and Josh. He punched in their birth years: 2-0-1-6-2-0-1-8. The keypad beeped and the safe clicked open.

Inside were three portable external solid-state drives—each about the size of a deck of cards with built-in USB cables—along with several USB thumb drives and a letter in an envelope addressed to him in his father's distinctive handwriting.

Atlas opened the letter with trembling hands and began to read:

"Atlas,

If you're reading this, I'm in trouble. Maybe dead. I hope not, but if these people are as dangerous as I think they are, it's a real possibility.

I've been investigating something called Project Genesis. It started as a routine insurance fraud case—a man named Robert Brooks died of an apparent heart attack, and his widow filed a life insurance claim. But when I started digging, I found something much bigger and much darker.

Project Genesis is an illegal genetic research program. They're experimenting on people, Atlas. Trying to create enhanced humans with superior physical and cognitive abilities. The experiments are brutal, often fatal, and conducted without consent on vulnerable people nobody will miss.

I've documented everything. The drives in this safe contain proof of murder, human experimentation, conspiracy at the highest levels. Names, dates, places, financial records. Everything needed to bring these people down.

But they found out I was investigating. They've threatened me, threatened your mother. I don't know what's going to happen, but I needed to make sure this evidence survived even if I don't.

If I'm gone, take these drives to the FBI. Ask for Agent Rachel Morrison—she's one of the few people I trust in law enforcement. She knows about Project Genesis, has been building her own case.

I'm sorry for dragging you into this. I'm sorry for the danger I've put our family in. But this is too important to ignore. These people are monsters, and someone has to stop them.

Tell your mother I love her. Tell Emma and Josh their grandpa loves them. And Atlas—I'm proud of you. Always have been, even if I didn't say it enough.

Keep your head down and trust no one.

—Dad"

Atlas's hands shook as he finished reading. His father had known he was in danger. Had known these people might kill him. And he'd tried to protect his family by hiding the evidence, by keeping them out of it.

But it hadn't worked.

"Atlas." Hollis's voice was urgent. She was looking at her phone, at a news alert that had just popped up. "Atlas, you need to see this."

She held out the phone. The headline made Atlas's world tilt:

"Local Man Found Dead in Apparent Homicide"

The article included a photo. Thomas Drummond, 68, found dead in his home this evening. Police are investigating the death as a homicide...

"No." The word came out as a whisper. "No, no, no. They said they had him. They said he was alive."

Hollis grabbed his shoulders. "Atlas, I'm so sorry. But we need to leave. Now. If they're willing to kill your father, they won't hesitate to come after you."

"My mother." Atlas looked at her, his eyes wild with grief and rage. "They still have my mother. Hollis, they still have my mother."

His phone rang. The same cultured voice from before.

"I'm sorry about your father, Mr. Drummond. He was... uncooperative. Refused to tell us where he'd hidden his evidence. Your mother, however, has been much more reasonable."

"Let me talk to her."

"Of course." A pause, then his mother's voice, stronger now but terrified.

"Atlas, don't trust them. They're going to kill me anyway. Don't give them—"

The line cut off.

"Forty-five hours and forty-one minutes, Mr. Drummond. Find the evidence and bring it to us. We'll be in touch with instructions."

The call ended.

Atlas stood in the storage unit, surrounded by his father's carefully accumulated evidence, and felt rage like he'd never experienced before. These people had killed his father. They were holding his mother hostage. And they thought they could threaten him into submission.

They were wrong.

"Hollis," Atlas said, his voice cold and hard. "I need you to copy everything on these drives. Multiple copies, different locations, cloud storage, dead-man switches—everything. If something happens to me, I want this evidence to automatically go out to every news organization and law enforcement agency in the country."

"Atlas—"

"They killed my father. They're going to try to kill my mother and me too. But I'm not going down without a fight." He picked up the portable SSDs and thumb drives, cradling them carefully. His father's last gift. His final act of defiance. "These people think they can operate in the shadows, that they can kill whoever they want with no consequences. We're going to prove them wrong."

"How?"

"I don't know yet. But we're going to find my mother, we're going to stop these people, and we're going to make sure the world knows what they did." Atlas looked at Hollis, saw his own determination reflected in her eyes. "Are you with me?"

Hollis didn't hesitate. "I'm with you. Whatever it takes."

They loaded the evidence into Atlas's truck and

drove away from the storage unit, both checking mirrors constantly, both expecting to be followed or ambushed at any moment.

But the streets were clear. Either their enemies didn't know about the storage unit yet, or they were waiting to see what Atlas would do next.

As they drove, Atlas's phone buzzed with a text from an unknown number:

"Check the files. Robert Brooks—your friend Hollis's father. Subject 47. He didn't die of natural causes."

Atlas's blood ran cold. He showed the message to Hollis.

She took the phone with shaking hands and read the message. Her face went pale.

"My father," she whispered. "What does that mean?"

"Let's find out." Atlas pulled into an empty parking lot behind a closed shopping center. "Hollis, open those files. Search for Robert Brooks."

Hollis pulled out her laptop and connected one of the portable SSDs using its built-in USB cable. Her fingers flew over the keyboard, searching through directories, opening files.

And then she found it.

A file labeled "Subject 47 - Robert Brooks."

She opened it, and they both read in silence. Medical records. Experimental protocols. Notes about genetic modifications and their effects. Test results. Progress reports written in cold, clinical language that treated human beings like laboratory equipment.

And finally, a death certificate with a note: " Subject 47 - Robert Brooks - Recruited through private research study advertising '$15,000 compensation for Performance Enhancement Trial' targeting fit veterans. Subject in excellent health, ideal baseline. Cardiac enhancement protocol administered over 6 weeks. Payment schedule: $15,000 upon study completion. Subject expired at home 3 days before final payment due. Death falsified as natural heart attack. Compensation never paid to family. Case closed."

Hollis's hands were shaking so badly she could barely hold the laptop.

"They killed him," she said, her voice barely audible. "They experimented on my father and killed him. And I never knew. All this time, I thought it was just a heart attack. That it was natural. But they murdered him."

Tears streamed down her face. Atlas took the laptop from her and set it aside, then pulled her into his arms. She sobbed against his chest, her body shaking with grief and rage.

"I'm so sorry," Atlas said quietly. "Hollis, I'm so sorry."

After a few minutes, Hollis pulled back, wiping her eyes. Her face was set with determination, all traces of tears gone except for the redness around her eyes.

"They're going to pay for this," she said, her voice hard as steel. "My father, your father, all the other victims. We're going to make them pay."

"Yes," Atlas agreed. "We are."

They sat in the dark parking lot for a long moment, both processing what they'd learned, both grieving for their fathers.

Then Atlas started the engine. "We need somewhere safe to go through these files. Somewhere they won't find us."

"I know a place," Hollis said. "A motel on the edge of town. The kind of place that takes cash and doesn't ask questions."

"Perfect."

They drove through the rain-soaked city, two people who'd met by chance just hours ago, now bound together by shared loss and common purpose.

The countdown continued: forty-five hours, twelve minutes.

But Atlas was done playing by their rules. His father had died gathering evidence against these monsters. Now it was Atlas's turn to finish what his father had started.

For his mother. For Hollis's father. For all the victims of Project Genesis.

This was war now.

And Atlas Drummond knew how to fight wars.

Chapter 3: Evidence And Allies

The Starlite Motel sat on the eastern edge of the city, a relic from the 1960s that had seen better days. Peeling paint, flickering neon sign, parking lot full of potholes. The kind of place where the clerk didn't look up from his phone when Atlas paid cash for a room, didn't ask for ID, didn't care why two people were checking in at three in the morning.

Room 117 smelled like cigarette smoke and industrial cleaner, but it had a deadbolt, a chain lock, and curtains thick enough to block any view from outside. Atlas checked the bathroom, looked under the bed, examined the window locks. Old habits.

"We're clear," he said, setting down the bag containing his father's portable SSDs and thumb drives.

Hollis was already setting up her laptop on the small table by the window, pulling out cables and adapters. "I'm going to start copying these files. It'll take a few hours to get everything uploaded to secure cloud storage."

"How secure are we talking?"

"Encrypted, distributed across multiple servers in

different countries, set up with dead-man switches that require me to check in every twelve hours or the files automatically release to a predetermined list of recipients." Hollis's fingers flew across the keyboard. "If something happens to either of us, the truth gets out."

Atlas sat on the edge of the bed, suddenly feeling the weight of the past few hours. His father was dead. His mother was being held hostage by people who'd already proven they were willing to kill. And he'd just met a woman in a bar who was now the only person he could trust.

"You should try to sleep," Hollis said without looking up from her screen. "You're going to need to be sharp tomorrow."

"I can't sleep. Not while my mother is out there."

"Then at least rest. Close your eyes for a few minutes." She glanced at him, her expression softening. "Atlas, I know what you're feeling. The guilt, the rage, the need to do something right now. But we can't help anyone if we're running on empty."

She was right, but that didn't make it easier. Atlas lay back on the bed, staring at the water-stained ceiling, listening to the click of Hollis's keyboard and the quiet hum of data transferring from the portable drives.

His phone sat on the nightstand, silent. Part of him wanted to call the number on that business card, demand to speak to his mother again, threaten them, make them understand that he wasn't going to roll over.

But that would be stupid. Emotional. The kind of mistake that got people killed.

He must have dozed off despite himself, because when he opened his eyes, pale morning light was filtering through the curtains. His phone showed 6:47 AM. He'd been asleep for about three hours.

Hollis was still at the table, still working, though she'd changed positions. Now she was reading through files on screen, taking notes on a legal pad.

"You didn't sleep at all?" Atlas asked, his voice rough.

"Couldn't. Too wired." She looked exhausted, dark circles under her eyes, but her gaze was sharp. "Besides, I wanted to go through some of these files. Atlas, what your father documented... it's worse than I imagined."

Atlas stood up, went to the bathroom to splash water on his face, then joined her at the table. "Show me."

Hollis pulled up a document—a spreadsheet with hundreds of entries. "This is a list of test subjects. Your father compiled it from medical records, death certificates, insurance claims. He cross-referenced everything, found patterns."

Atlas scanned the list. Names, ages, dates, causes of death. Robert Brooks, Subject 47. But there were dozens of others. Hundreds.

"How many?" he asked quietly.

"As far as I can tell, at least two hundred and thirty subjects over the past ten years. Maybe more—these are just the ones your father could document." Hollis clicked to another file. "Most of them were vulnerable people. Homeless individuals, undocumented immigrants, people with no families to ask questions. A few were like my father—people who died of 'natural causes' that weren't natural at all."

"Who's running this? Who's behind Project Genesis?"

Hollis pulled up another document. "According to your father's notes, the operation is run by Dr. Lawrence Ashford. He's a geneticist, formerly worked at several major universities before being fired for ethical violations. Now he runs what's supposedly a private research facility."

A photo appeared on screen—a man in his early seventies, distinguished-looking with silver hair and cold eyes.

"Where's this facility?"

"That's the problem. Your father couldn't find it. He knew it existed, had evidence of the experiments, but he couldn't pin down a physical location." Hollis clicked through more files. "What he did find was the money trail. Project Genesis is funded by something called Helix Innovations—a biotech company with billions in assets."

"So we go after Helix."

"It's not that simple. Helix is publicly traded, seemingly legitimate. On paper, they do normal genetic research. But your father believed they were using Project Genesis as their illegal testing ground, doing experiments they couldn't do through official channels."

Atlas studied the files, the evidence his father had died gathering. "Agent Rachel Morrison. My father mentioned her in his letter. Said she was FBI, building her own case."

"I found references to her in the files too." Hollis pulled up an email chain—encrypted communications between Thomas Drummond and someone with the email address RMorrison@fbi.gov. "Looks like your father had been working with her for at least three months. She was investigating Project Genesis from the law enforcement side while he gathered evidence from the insurance angle."

"Then we contact her. Give her everything my father found."

"And your mother? These people said they'd know if you involved law enforcement."

Atlas's jaw tightened. That was the impossible choice. Follow his father's instructions and go to the FBI, potentially saving hundreds of lives but risking his mother's. Or try to handle this alone, maybe save his mother but let Project Genesis continue operating.

"Let me think about it," he said finally. "What else did you find?"

Hollis pulled up another file, this one containing photographs. "These are from inside one of the facilities. Your father must have gotten them from a source—maybe someone who worked there and got scared."

The images made Atlas's stomach turn. Laboratory rooms with medical equipment. Holding cells that looked more like prison than hospital. And people—test subjects in various states of suffering. Emaciated, scarred, some barely conscious.

"Jesus," Atlas breathed.

"There's more." Hollis's voice was tight. "Look at this one."

She zoomed in on a photograph of a whiteboard covered in scientific notation and medical terminology. But in the corner, someone had written a list of names and numbers.

One of them was "R. Brooks - Subject 47 - Cardiac enhancement protocol - EXPIRED."

Hollis's hand trembled as she pointed at her father's name. "That's what they called him. Not a person. Not a Marine who served his country. Just Subject 47."

Atlas put his hand over hers. "We're going to make them pay for this. All of it."

His phone rang. Unknown number, but not the one that had called before.

Atlas answered cautiously. "Hello?"

"Mr. Drummond?" A woman's voice, professional and urgent. "This is Agent Rachel Morrison, FBI. I've been trying to reach your father for the past two days. When I couldn't get through, I started making calls. I just learned about his death."

A pause. "I'm so sorry for your loss. Your father was a brave man."

Atlas looked at Hollis, who was listening intently. "How did you get this number?"

"Your father gave it to me months ago as an emergency contact. He said if anything happened to him, I should reach out to you." Morrison's voice was steady. "Mr. Drummond, I know this is a lot to process, but I need to know—did your father have time to secure his evidence before he was killed? The files he was compiling about Project Genesis?"

"Why should I trust you?"

"Because I've been investigating Project Genesis for two years. Because I've put my career on the line trying to expose what's happening. And because right now, you're in serious danger and I might be the only person who can help you."

Atlas made a decision. "I have the files. My father left them for me."

"Thank God." Morrison's relief was audible. "Are you somewhere safe?"

"For now."

"We need to meet. Today. I can bring you into protective custody, keep you safe while we—"

"They have my mother," Atlas interrupted. "The people behind Project Genesis. They're holding her hostage. They said if I involve law enforcement, she dies."

Morrison was quiet for a moment. "When did they take her?"

"Last night. They gave me forty-eight hours to hand over my father's evidence. I have..." Atlas checked his phone. "About forty-two hours left."

"Okay. Okay, listen to me carefully. Don't try to make the exchange. These people will kill both you and your mother the moment they have the evidence. Your only chance is to let me help you."

"How? You just said you've been investigating for two years. If you could have stopped them, you would have already."

"Because I didn't have what your father had. I had pieces—witness testimony, partial financial records, circumstantial evidence. But I didn't have proof. The kind of evidence that would stand up in court and justify raiding their facilities." Morrison's voice was intense. "Mr. Drummond, with what your father compiled, I can get warrants. I can mobilize tactical teams. I can shut down Project Genesis and rescue your mother."

"And if you can't? If something goes wrong?"

"Then we're no worse off than we are now. But if you try to handle this alone, you will die. I've seen what these people do to threats. Your father wasn't the first person they've killed, and he won't be the last."

Atlas looked at Hollis. She was shaking her head, writing something on her legal pad: Don't trust anyone. Not yet.

"I need time to think," Atlas said.

"You don't have time. Every hour we wait is an hour they're moving assets, destroying evidence, preparing to disappear." Morrison paused. "I understand you don't know me. You have no reason to trust me. So I'm going to tell you something that's classified, something that could end my career. Three months ago, I planted an undercover agent inside Helix Innovations. He's been feeding me information, confirming what your father found. But two weeks ago, he went dark. I think they discovered him. I think he's dead."

"What was his name?"

"Ryan Foster. Twenty-eight years old. Engaged to

be married. Good man, good agent." Morrison's voice cracked slightly. "I sent him in there, and now he's gone. So believe me when I say I understand what you're risking. But we have a chance here—maybe our only chance—to shut these people down and save the people they're still holding. Including your mother."

Atlas closed his eyes, weighing options. Every instinct told him not to trust anyone, to handle this himself. But he wasn't stupid. He was a former soldier, not some action hero. He didn't have the resources, the manpower, or the expertise to take on an organization this big and this connected.

"Where do you want to meet?" he asked.

"There's a diner on Route 7, about thirty miles outside the city. Maggie's. Can you be there in two hours?"

"I'll be there."

"Come alone. And Mr. Drummond? Watch for tails. If they're monitoring you, lead them away from your evidence before you come to meet me."

The call ended.

"You're really going to trust her?" Hollis asked.

"I don't know. But she's right about one thing—we can't do this alone." Atlas started gathering the portable drives. "We need to split up the evidence. Keep some copies with us, hide others in different locations. That way if something happens—"

"The truth still gets out. I'm already on it." Hollis held up three USB thumb drives. "These are encrypted copies of everything. I'm going to mail one to a lawyer I trust in Atlanta, hide one in a safety deposit box under a false name, and keep one with me."

"Smart."

"I'm also setting up the dead-man switch. If I don't check in every twelve hours, everything gets released to the media, FBI, Justice Department, every major news organization in the country."

Atlas looked at her, this woman who'd walked into a bar less than twelve hours ago, who'd had every reason to walk away but had chosen to stay and fight. "Why are you doing this? You could have left. You could have taken what you learned about your father and just... walked away."

"Because my father was murdered. Because two hundred and thirty other people were murdered or tortured. Because if we don't stop this, it'll keep happening." Hollis met his eyes. "And because you need help, and I'm in a position to give it. That's enough."

Atlas's phone buzzed. A text from Sarah: "Is everything okay? You were supposed to pick up Emma and Josh this morning. They're worried about you."

He'd completely forgotten. This was supposed to be his weekend with the kids.

He called Sarah, got her voicemail. Left a message: "Sarah, I'm sorry. There's a family emergency. My father died last night. I can't take the kids this weekend. I'll explain everything later, but please tell Emma and Josh that I love them and I'll see them as soon as I can."

He hung up, feeling like the worst father in the world. But bringing his kids anywhere near this situation would be insane.

"You should eat something," Hollis said, practical as always. "We've got time before your meeting with Morrison. There's a diner across the street."

They went to the diner, a greasy spoon called Pete's that served all-day breakfast. Atlas ordered coffee and scrambled eggs he couldn't taste. Hollis got pancakes she didn't eat. Both of them kept watching the door, scanning faces, looking for threats.

"Tell me about your kids," Hollis said, clearly trying to focus on something normal.

"Emma's nine. Smart as hell, wants to be a lawyer. Reads constantly, usually three or four books ahead of her grade level." Atlas smiled despite everything. "Josh is seven. Complete opposite—all energy, all the time. Obsessed with dinosaurs and superheroes. Can't sit still for more than five minutes."

"They sound wonderful."

"They are. They're the best thing I ever did." Atlas's smile faded. "I'm terrified this is going to touch them somehow. That these people will use them to get to me."

"They won't. We won't let them."

Atlas's phone buzzed again. Another text, this time from the number that had threatened him last night:

"We know you found your father's storage unit. We know you have the evidence. But here's what you don't know, Mr. Drummond—we also have your ex-wife and children. They're safe right now. Whether they stay safe depends on your cooperation. You have 41 hours, 23 minutes remaining. Tick tock."

Atlas's blood turned to ice. He showed Hollis the

message.

"No," she breathed. "No, they can't—"

Atlas was already calling Sarah. Straight to voicemail.

He called Emma's phone—the cell phone he'd gotten her for emergencies. Voicemail.

He called the house phone. Nothing.

"We need to go," Atlas said, throwing money on the table. "Now."

They ran to the truck. Atlas drove too fast, his mind racing through scenarios, each one worse than the last. Sarah's house was fifteen minutes away. Fifteen minutes that felt like hours.

Please let them be okay. Please let them be okay. Please let them be okay.

He kept trying to call, kept getting voicemail. The terror was overwhelming, threatening to shut down his ability to think.

"They might be fine," Hollis said, though she didn't sound convinced. "The message could be a bluff. They might be trying to panic you into making a mistake."

"Or they might have my children."

Sarah's house looked normal from the outside. Her car in the driveway. Curtains open. Nothing obviously wrong.

But when Atlas used his emergency key to open the front door, he found the house empty. No Sarah. No Emma. No Josh.

And on the Kitchen table, a note written in block letters:

"MAKE THE EXCHANGE, OR THEY DIE. ALL OF THEM. 41 HOURS."

Atlas stood in his ex-wife's Kitchen, surrounded by the life she'd built after their marriage ended, and felt the world collapsing around him.

They had his mother. They had Sarah. They had Emma and Josh.

And he had forty-one hours to figure out how to save them all.

He walked through the house in a daze, checking rooms, looking for any sign of struggle. Emma's room was neat, her bed made, her stuffed animals arranged on the pillow the way she always left them. Josh's room was chaotic as always, toys everywhere, dinosaur posters on the walls.

Everything normal. Everything wrong.

In Sarah's bedroom, Atlas found her phone on the nightstand. Dead battery. That's why she hadn't answered. But where was she? Where were the kids?

His own phone rang. The cultured voice again.

"Mr. Drummond. I see you've discovered our expanded accommodations."

"If you hurt them—" Atlas's voice was raw with rage and fear.

"They're unharmed. Your children are actually quite entertaining. The boy won't stop talking about dinosaurs. The girl keeps asking when her father is coming to get her." A pause, letting that sink in. "They trust you'll save them, Mr. Drummond. Don't disappoint them."

"Let me talk to them."

"No. Not until you've demonstrated cooperation. You have the evidence. Bring it to us. All of it. Do that, and you get your family back."

"How do I know—"

"You don't. But consider your alternatives. You can trust that we'll honor the exchange, or you can watch everyone you love die. Starting with your children." The voice was cold, matter-of-fact. "The meeting location will be sent to you in thirty-six hours. Until then, Mr. Drummond, I suggest you think very carefully about your choices."

The line went dead.

Atlas stood in his ex-wife's bedroom, phone still pressed to his ear, everything he cared about held hostage by monsters.

Hollis appeared in the doorway. "Atlas, we should go. The neighbors might have seen us, might call the police. We can't be here when they show up."

She was right. But Atlas couldn't move. Couldn't process what was happening.

Emma asking when her father was coming. Josh talking about dinosaurs like everything was normal. Sarah taken because of him, because of his father's investigation, because Atlas had gotten involved.

"Atlas." Hollis's voice was firm now. She grabbed his arm. "We have to go. Right now. We'll figure out how to save them, but we can't do it from a police

interrogation room."

That penetrated the fog. Atlas let Hollis lead him out of the house, back to his truck. She drove this time, Atlas too shaken to focus.

"Where are we going?" he asked dully.

"Back to the motel. We need to regroup, think this through." Hollis's jaw was set with determination. "They have your family, Atlas. But we have something they need. That gives us leverage."

"They'll kill them."

"Not if we're smart. Not if we use what we have." She glanced at him. "Your meeting with Morrison—you still need to go. She's FBI. She has resources. Maybe she can help find where they're holding your family."

"Or maybe she's compromised. Maybe she's working with them."

"Then we find out. But doing nothing isn't an option."

Atlas looked at the clock on his dashboard. 8:47 AM, Friday, October 24, 2025. He had less than forty-one hours until the deadline. Forty-one hours to save his mother, his ex-wife, and his two children from people

who'd already proven they were willing to kill.

The meeting with Morrison was at 10:00 AM. Less than two hours away.

"What do we bring to the meeting?" Atlas asked. "We can't bring the original drives. If she's dirty, we lose everything."

"We bring copies on a thumb drive. Enough to prove we have what she needs, not enough to give everything away." Hollis was thinking tactically now. "And we don't tell her about your family being taken. Not yet. Not until we know we can trust her."

"Agreed."

They drove back to the Starlite Motel in silence. Atlas's mind was racing through scenarios, trying to find a way out of this trap. But every path he saw led to death—his family's or his own or both.

Back in the motel room, Hollis prepared a sample thumb drive while Atlas sat on the bed, head in his hands.

"I should have known," he said quietly. "Should have realized they'd go after Sarah and the kids. Should have gotten them to safety."

"You couldn't have known. None of us could."

Hollis sat beside him. "Atlas, look at me."

He looked up. Her green eyes were steady, fierce.

"We're going to save them. All of them. Your mother, Sarah, Emma, Josh. We're going to get them back, and we're going to destroy the people who did this." She took his hand. "But I need you to stay focused. Can you do that?"

"I don't know."

"Yes, you do. You're a soldier. You've been in impossible situations before. You know how to push through fear and think tactically." She squeezed his hand. "Your kids need their father. Not the scared, broken version. The strong one who doesn't quit."

Atlas took a deep breath, then another. She was right. Falling apart wouldn't save anyone. He needed to think, to plan, to use every skill he'd learned in the Army.

"Okay," he said. "Okay. What's our play?"

"We go to the meeting with Morrison. We feel her out, see if we can trust her. If she's legitimate, we bring her in on this—use FBI resources to find where they're holding your family. If she's dirty or compromised, we walk away and figure out plan B."

"And if there is no plan B?"

"Then we make one up. We improvise. We do whatever it takes." Hollis stood up. "Come on. We need to leave for the meeting in thirty minutes. You should clean up, change clothes. Look like someone in control."

Atlas went through the motions—shower, fresh clothes from the bag he kept in his truck, checking his weapons. The familiar routine helped center him, gave him something concrete to focus on.

When they were ready to leave, Hollis handed him the thumb drive. "Sample files. Enough to prove we have the real evidence, not enough to give them everything. Don't let it out of your sight."

"What about you? You're not coming?"

"I'm staying here with the original drives. If something goes wrong at your meeting, if you don't come back, I'll know to activate the dead-man switches and get out." Hollis held his gaze. "But you're coming back, Atlas. You hear me? You're coming back, and then we're going to save your family."

Atlas pulled her into a brief, fierce hug. "Thank you. For all of this. For staying when you could have run."

"We're partners now. Partners don't run." She pulled back. "Now go. And Atlas? Trust your instincts. If something feels wrong about Morrison, it probably is."

Atlas drove toward Route 7, toward Maggie's Diner, toward what might be salvation or another trap. The morning was clear and cold, October sunshine doing nothing to warm the chill in his bones.

He checked his mirrors constantly, looking for tails. Saw nothing obvious, but that didn't mean they weren't there. These people had resources, had proven they could watch him without being seen.

The diner appeared after twenty-five minutes of driving—a classic roadside establishment with chrome trim and a neon sign. The parking lot was half full, morning breakfast crowd lingering over coffee.

Atlas parked where he could see the entrance, watched for ten minutes before going in. Looking for anything suspicious, any sign this was a setup.

He saw nothing. Just regular people having breakfast, living normal lives, unaware of the nightmare Atlas was trapped in.

Finally, he got out of the truck and went inside.

The diner was warm, smelled like bacon and coffee. A hostess started to approach him, but Atlas spotted Agent Rachel Morrison in a back booth and headed toward her.

She stood as he approached. Mid-forties, dark hair cut short, sharp eyes that assessed him quickly. She wore jeans and a blazer, trying to look casual but radiating law enforcement.

"Mr. Drummond." She extended her hand. "Thank you for coming."

Atlas shook her hand, noting the firm grip, the calluses that suggested she spent time at the range. He slid into the booth across from her.

"Did you come alone?" Morrison asked.

"Did you?"

She smiled slightly. "I have a partner in a car outside. Standard protocol. You can't be too careful."

"No. You can't." Atlas studied her face, trying to read her. Was she trustworthy? Compromised? Playing both sides?

A waitress appeared. Morrison ordered coffee. Atlas did the same, though he didn't plan to drink it.

When the waitress left, Morrison leaned forward. "I need to know what you have. Your father told me he was close to having everything documented, but we didn't get a chance to meet before he was killed."

"Why should I trust you?"

"Because I've been investigating Project Genesis for two years. Because I've put my career on the line trying to expose it. Because your father trusted me, and that should count for something." Morrison's eyes were steady. "I know you're scared. I know you don't know who to trust. But Mr. Drummond—Atlas—I'm one of the good guys. Let me help you."

Atlas reached into his pocket, pulled out the thumb drive. Set it on the table between them.

"Sample files. Proof that I have what you need. Names, dates, evidence of human experimentation and murder. Everything my father compiled."

Morrison picked up the thumb drive, turning it over in her hands like it was precious. Which it was. "And the rest?"

"Somewhere safe. If you're legitimate, if you can help me, you'll get it all. But I need guarantees first."

"What kind of guarantees?"

This was the moment. Atlas had to decide—tell her about his family being taken, or keep that card close to his chest.

He made a choice.

"I need to know you can shut down Project Genesis. All of it. I need to know the people responsible will face justice. And I need to know you can do it quickly."

"Why quickly?"

"Because people are still in danger. Because every day we wait is another day these people can destroy evidence, hurt more victims, disappear."

Morrison studied him. "There's something you're not telling me."

"There's a lot I'm not telling you. Until I know I can trust you."

A long pause. Then Morrison nodded. "Fair enough. Here's what I can offer. You give me the full evidence, I'll have warrants within twenty-four hours. We'll raid every location connected to Project Genesis, arrest everyone involved, shut the whole operation down. Federal charges, maximum sentences. These people will never see daylight again."

"Can you guarantee that?"

"In law enforcement, there are no guarantees. But I can promise I'll use every resource at my disposal to make it happen." Morrison leaned forward. "Your father spent six months gathering this evidence. He died for it. Don't let that be for nothing."

Atlas wanted to believe her. Wanted to think the FBI could swoop in and solve everything, save his family, make the nightmare end.

But he'd learned the hard way that the system didn't always work. That sometimes the good guys lost.

"I need time to think," Atlas said, starting to stand up.

"Wait." Morrison pulled out a folder, slid it across the table. "Before you go, look at this."

Atlas opened the folder. Inside were photographs. Crime scene photos, medical examiner reports, death certificates.

All victims of Project Genesis. Men, women, some barely adults. All dead. All with the same falsified causes of death—heart attacks, accidents, natural causes.

"Two hundred and thirty people," Morrison said

quietly. "That we know of. There are probably more. All of them experimented on. All of them dead or permanently damaged. And the people responsible are still out there, still operating, still hurting people."

She pulled out another photo. This one showed a young man in an FBI jacket, smiling at the camera. "Ryan Foster. The agent I sent undercover. He was twenty-eight years old. Engaged to a woman named Jessica. They were planning a wedding for next spring." Morrison's voice was tight. "He went dark two weeks ago. We found his body yesterday, dumped in a warehouse. They'd tortured him before they killed him."

Atlas looked at the photo. Ryan Foster had kind eyes, a good smile. Someone's fiancé. Someone's son. Dead because he'd tried to stop Project Genesis.

"I'm telling you this because I want you to understand what we're up against," Morrison said. "These people are ruthless. They will kill anyone who threatens them. And right now, you're a threat. The evidence you have makes you the biggest threat they've ever faced."

"I know."

"Then you know you can't do this alone. You need help. You need resources. You need me." Morrison closed the folder. "I'm not asking you to trust me completely. I'm asking you to trust me enough to let me help. Give me the evidence. Let me do my job. Let's finish what your father started."

Atlas sat back down. Everything Morrison was saying made sense. But sense didn't mean truth.

"If I give you the evidence, what happens to me?"

"Protective custody until we shut down Project Genesis. Then you testify at the trials. After that, you're free to resume your life."

"And if something goes wrong? If they have people inside the FBI, like they claim?"

"Then we're all screwed." Morrison's bluntness was almost refreshing. "But I've been careful. I've kept my investigation compartmentalized. Only a handful of people know about it. The risk is manageable."

"Manageable." Atlas laughed bitterly. "My father thought the risk was manageable too. Now he's dead."

Morrison's expression softened. "I know. I'm sorry. Your father was a good man, and he didn't deserve what happened to him. But hiding won't bring him back. And it won't stop Project Genesis."

Atlas's phone buzzed. A text from Hollis:

"Everything okay?"

He typed back: "Still talking. Need more time."

"Someone waiting for you?" Morrison asked.

"A friend."

"The woman from the bar. Hollis Brooks." Morrison saw Atlas's expression and held up a hand. "I've been keeping tabs on you since your father died. Standard protocol. I know you met her at McGinty's Bar Thursday night, that she followed you to your apartment, that you've been together since. Hollis Brooks, 30, IT security consultant, daughter of Robert Brooks who died five years ago of a supposed heart attack."

"You've been watching me."

"Protecting you. There's a difference." Morrison pulled out another photo, this one showing the black SUV from the parking lot. "We've identified this vehicle as belonging to a private security firm called Aegis Solutions. They're known to do wet work for wealthy clients. The man who approached you is named Victor Kozlov. Former Russian military, now a hired gun."

Atlas stared at the photo. The man who'd threatened him had a name now. Victor Kozlov.

"We're watching him too," Morrison continued. "And we're watching several other known operatives connected to Project Genesis. The moment you give me the evidence and we get warrants, we'll move on all of them simultaneously. Fast, coordinated, overwhelming force. They won't see it coming."

It sounded good. It sounded like exactly what Atlas needed.

But something still felt off. Something Atlas couldn't quite identify.

"I need to think about this," he said again. "Give me until tonight. I'll call you with my decision."

Morrison looked frustrated but nodded. "Tonight. But Atlas? Don't wait too long. These people are getting nervous. Nervous people make mistakes, and mistakes get people killed."

Atlas stood up. "I'll be in touch." He left the thumb drive on the table. Morrison could review the sample files, verify they were real. But she wouldn't get the rest until he decided he could trust her.

He walked out of the diner, got into his truck, and drove away. In his rearview mirror, he saw Morrison talking on her phone, her expression worried.

Was she calling her FBI partner? Or was she calling someone else? Someone in Project Genesis, warning them that Atlas Drummond had the evidence and needed to be eliminated?

Atlas didn't know. Couldn't know.

All he knew was that in less than forty hours, he had to make an exchange that would determine whether his family lived or died.

And he still had no idea how to save them all.

Chapter 4: Paranoia And Planning

Atlas drove away from Maggie's Diner, checking his mirrors every few seconds. No obvious tail, but that meant nothing. These people had followed him before without him noticing until they wanted to be seen.

His phone rang. Hollis.

"How'd it go?" she asked.

"I don't know. She seemed legitimate. Said all the right things." Atlas took a random turn, still checking mirrors. "But something felt off. I can't explain it."

"Trust your gut. Your gut has kept you alive this long."

"I left her the sample thumb drive. She can verify the files are real, see what we have. But I didn't commit to anything."

"Good. Come back to the motel. We need to figure out our next move."

Atlas took a circuitous route back, adding an extra twenty minutes to make sure he wasn't followed. When he finally pulled into the Starlite Motel parking lot, he sat in his truck for five minutes, watching, waiting.

Nothing.

Inside room 117, Hollis had the curtains drawn and her laptop open. The portable SSDs sat on the table beside her, innocuous-looking devices that held evidence of mass murder.

"I've been going through more files," Hollis said without preamble. "Your father documented everything, Atlas. Not just the victims and the experiments, but the entire organizational structure. He found the money trail, identified key players, even mapped out relationships between Project Genesis and legitimate companies."

"Show me."

Hollis pulled up a diagram on her screen—a complex web of connections. At the center was Helix Innovations. Radiating outward were dozens of shell companies, research facilities, and individuals.

"Dr. Lawrence Ashford runs the operation," Hollis said, pointing to a photo. "But he's not the money. That comes from here." She highlighted a name at the top of the chart. "Edmund Carver. Billionaire, owns Helix Innovations, has his fingers in a dozen different biotech companies."

Atlas studied the photo of Edmund Carver—late

sixties, patrician features, the kind of man who looked like he belonged on the cover of Forbes. "Why would a billionaire fund illegal human experiments?"

"According to your father's notes, Carver has pancreatic cancer. Stage four. He's dying." Hollis clicked through more files. "Your father theorized that Carver was funding Project Genesis to find a cure for himself. The genetic enhancements, the experiments—they were all aimed at developing treatments that could save him."

"So two hundred and thirty people died so one rich guy could try to cheat death."

"Essentially, yes." Hollis's voice was bitter. "My father was just a lab rat to them. A test subject they could use to see if their treatments worked before they tried them on someone who mattered."

Atlas put his hand on her shoulder. "Your father mattered. All of them mattered."

"I know. But they didn't see it that way." Hollis took a breath, visibly pulling herself together. "There's more. Your father identified at least six different facilities where Project Genesis operates. Three in the US, one in Mexico, two in South America. The main facility—the one where Ashford works—is somewhere in the US, but your father couldn't pin down the exact location."

"Morrison said she could get warrants, shut everything down. If we give her the full evidence."

"Do you trust her?"

"I want to. But my father trusted the system, and it got him killed." Atlas sat down on the bed, suddenly exhausted. "I don't know what to do, Hollis. Every option feels like a trap."

"Then let's think it through systematically." Hollis pulled out her legal pad, started writing. "Option one: We give Morrison everything. She gets warrants, raids the facilities, arrests everyone involved. Best case scenario, she's legitimate and we shut down Project Genesis. Worst case, she's compromised and we've handed our only leverage to the enemy."

"But even if she's legitimate, the moment raids start, they'll kill the hostages. My family would be dead before the first arrest is made."

Hollis stopped writing, her pen hovering over the paper. "You're right. I didn't think about that."

"So working with the FBI isn't an option. Not while they have my family." Atlas stood up, started pacing. "What else?"

"Option two: We try to make the exchange

ourselves. Trade the evidence for your family. Best case, they honor the deal and everyone goes free. Worst case—and most likely case—they kill all of us and take the evidence anyway."

"Option three?"

"We go public. Release everything to the media, law enforcement, everyone. Force the issue into the open where they can't hide." Hollis looked up from her notes. "Best case, public pressure forces action and your family gets rescued in the chaos. Worst case, they kill your family immediately to eliminate witnesses, and we spend the rest of our lives looking over our shoulders."

Atlas rubbed his face. "Those are all terrible options."

"I know. But they're the options we have." Hollis set down her pen. "What do your instincts tell you?"

Atlas thought about it. "My instincts tell me that we can't rely on anyone but ourselves. Morrison might be legitimate, but even if she is, she can't move fast enough. The FBI has procedures, protocols, chains of command. By the time they get warrants and mobilize teams, my family could be dead."

"So we handle it ourselves."

"We handle it ourselves." Atlas pulled out his phone. "I have friends. Military guys, people who know how to handle themselves in a fight. If I can get them on board, we could have a team in place when the exchange goes down."

"That's incredibly dangerous."

"More dangerous than trusting a system that's already failed? More dangerous than handing over our only leverage and hoping they don't kill us all?" Atlas stopped pacing. "Hollis, these people don't play fair. The only way to beat them is to be more prepared than they expect."

Hollis was quiet for a long moment. Then she nodded. "Okay. But if we're doing this, we do it smart. We plan every detail. We have contingencies for the contingencies. And we make sure that even if everything goes wrong, the truth still gets out."

"The dead-man switch."

"Exactly. I need to do my twelve-hour check-in at three PM anyway. I'll make sure everything's locked in—if I miss a check-in, if anything happens to either of us, everything releases automatically."

Atlas checked his phone. 11:15 AM. Less than four

hours until Hollis's first check-in. Less than thirty-seven hours until the exchange deadline.

"Call your friends," Hollis said. "See who's willing to help. I'll keep working on the files, organize everything so we can release it all the moment your family is safe."

Over the next hour, Atlas made calls. He explained the situation in broad strokes—his father murdered, his family kidnapped, a criminal organization that needed to be taken down. He was careful not to mention Project Genesis specifically, not over potentially monitored phone lines.

Rodriguez was in. Marcus was in. Davis was in. Torres said he'd have to think about it, but Atlas heard in his voice that he'd come through.

"We need to meet," Rodriguez said. "Plan this properly. You got a location?"

Atlas gave him the address of a warehouse Marcus owned on the industrial side of town. "Six PM tonight. Come ready to work."

"Roger that. And Ace? Whatever this is, we've got your back."

After the calls were done, Atlas felt something he hadn't felt since this nightmare started: hope. Not much, not enough to be confident, but a flicker. He wasn't alone. He had allies, resources, a plan starting to form.

Hollis was watching him. "They're coming?"

"Yeah. Four guys, maybe five. All with combat experience. All willing to go outside the system."

"That's good. That's really good." Hollis glanced at the clock. "We should get burner phones. If they're tracking us through our cells, we need clean communication."

"There's a convenience store two blocks from here. I saw it on the way in." Atlas started to stand, but Hollis waved him back down.

"I'll go. You should rest - you only got a few hours sleep and you'll need more. I'll rest later."

She grabbed her jacket. "I'll be back in twenty minutes. Lock the door behind me, don't answer for anyone but me."

After Hollis left, Atlas sat on the bed, staring at the ceiling. His body was exhausted but his mind wouldn't stop racing. Emma and Josh, held somewhere by people who'd already proven they were willing to kill children. His mother, his ex-wife —all of them depending on him to save them.

And he had less than thirty-seven hours to figure out how.

His old phone—the one he knew might be compromised—sat on the nightstand. Atlas stared at it, then made a decision. He powered it up one last time to check for messages.

Immediately, three texts came through. All from the same unknown number.

"Tick tock, Mr. Drummond. 36 hours, 42 minutes."

"Your children are asking about you. The boy is crying. The girl is trying to be brave. How much longer will you make them wait?"

"We're watching you. We know about your military friends. Don't be stupid. Make the exchange, get your family back. It's the only way everyone survives."

Atlas's hands tightened on the phone. They'd been watching him make calls. They knew about Rodriguez and the others. Which meant either they had surveillance on the motel, or they'd tapped his phone.

Another text came through:

"We'll send you the exchange location in 24 hours.

Come alone. Bring all the evidence—we'll know if you hold anything back. Do this right, and by Sunday morning you'll have your family back. Do it wrong, and you'll be burying them."

Atlas took screenshots of the messages, then powered down the phone and removed the battery. When Hollis got back with the burners, this phone was going in the trash.

He lay back on the bed, closed his eyes. Just for a minute. Just to rest them.

He woke to Hollis shaking his shoulder. "Atlas. You need to see this."

He sat up, disoriented. The room was darker—the sun had moved. "What time is it?"

"Two forty-five. You've been asleep for over three hours." Hollis's face was pale. She held up her phone, showing a news alert. "There's been an explosion. At the FBI field office downtown."

Atlas grabbed the phone, read the breaking news alert. An explosion at the FBI building. Multiple casualties. No details yet on victims.

"Turn on the TV," Hollis said, her voice tight.

Atlas grabbed the remote, flipped to a news channel. A reporter stood in front of a building Atlas recognized—the FBI field office.

"—explosion occurred approximately thirty minutes ago," the reporter was saying. "FBI officials are confirming that Agent Rachel Morrison was killed in the blast, along with two other agents. Authorities are investigating this as a terrorist attack, though no group has claimed responsibility. The FBI is asking anyone with information to—"

Atlas muted the TV. Stared at the screen showing emergency vehicles, crime scene tape, the shattered entrance of the FBI building.

Agent Rachel Morrison was dead.

The only FBI agent who knew about Project Genesis, who'd been building a case, who Atlas had met with this morning.

Dead.

"It's not a coincidence," Hollis said quietly. "They killed her. Right after you gave her that sample thumb drive."

"Which means they were watching the diner. Watching us." Atlas felt cold spreading through his chest.

"Which means they know you're helping me."

"Then I'm already a target. We both are." Hollis sat down beside him. "Atlas, this changes everything. Morrison was our potential backup if things went wrong. Without her—"

"We're completely on our own." Atlas stood up, started pacing. "They killed her to send a message. To show us that no one can help us. That involving law enforcement gets people killed."

"Or they killed her because she was actually legitimate and they couldn't risk her building a case against them." Hollis's expression was grim. "Either way, we can't rely on the FBI now. Even if there are other good agents, we don't know who they are. We can't trust anyone in law enforcement."

Atlas's mind was racing. Morrison dead. No FBI backup. No legitimate path to stopping Project

Genesis. Just him, Hollis, and a handful of friends who were walking into a war.

"Your check-in," Atlas said, checking his watch. "You need to do it now, make sure the dead-man switch doesn't trigger."

Hollis opened her laptop, pulled up an encrypted

page. She entered a long password, clicked through several security screens. "Check-in complete. Next one due at 3:00 AM tomorrow."

"Lock it in. Make sure if anything happens to either of us, everything releases. Morrison's death proves they'll kill anyone who threatens them. Our only leverage is that they can't kill us without the evidence going public."

"Already locked in." Hollis closed her laptop. "But Atlas, we need to talk about the reality here. They have your family. They've proven they're willing to kill FBI agents. When the exchange happens, they're going to try to kill all of us—you, me, your family, anyone who knows anything."

"I know."

"So what's the plan? Really? Because going in there with four or five of your military buddies against a well-funded criminal organization with unlimited resources—those aren't good odds."

"Then we make better odds." Atlas pulled out one of the new burner phones Hollis had bought. "We contact Carver directly. Go over Ashford's head, talk to the man who's really running this."

"How do we even reach him?"

"Your father's files. There has to be contact information, phone numbers, addresses. Something we can use." Atlas was thinking tactically now, planning like he used to plan missions in Afghanistan. "We reach out to Carver, we tell him we want to negotiate directly with him. Cut out the middlemen, make a clean exchange."

"And you think he'll go for that?"

"He's dying. He's desperate. And he knows that if we release the evidence, his entire empire collapses. He goes to prison, loses everything, dies behind bars." Atlas met her eyes. "We offer him a deal. We give him the evidence in exchange for my family. He destroys it, we never speak of Project Genesis again, everyone walks away."

"You'd let him get away with it? After everything he's done?"

"No. But I'd let him think I would." Atlas pulled up the files on Hollis's laptop. "We make the deal, we get my family to safety, and then we release everything anyway. The dead-man switch triggers, or we do it manually. Either way, the truth gets out."

Hollis thought about it. "It's risky. He might not

believe you'd really let him walk away."

"Then we make him believe it. We give him just enough to think he's won." Atlas found what he was looking for—a file containing phone numbers, including one labeled "EC - Private Line." Edmund Carver's direct number.

"What if he doesn't answer?"

"Then we leave a message. A very clear message that we're willing to deal." Atlas picked up the burner phone. "But we do this on our terms, not his."

Before he could dial, Hollis grabbed his hand. "Wait. If we do this, if we contact him directly, there's no going back. We're committing to a path that ends with us either saving your family or getting everyone killed."

"I know."

"And you're okay with that?"

Atlas thought about Emma asking when her father was coming. Josh crying. His mother, his ex-wife, all of them depending on him.

"I don't have a choice," he said. "They made this personal when they took my family. Now I'm going to end it."

He dialed the number.

It rang three times. Then a voice answered—cultured, slightly accented, exactly like the voice that had threatened him before.

"Mr. Drummond. I've been expecting your call."

"Edmund Carver?"

"The same. And let me save us both some time. Yes, I'm the one behind Project Genesis. Yes, I have your family. Yes, I will kill them if you don't cooperate. Now, what do you want to say that's worth calling me directly?"

Atlas took a breath. "I want to make a deal."

"I'm listening."

"You want the evidence my father collected. I want my family back alive and unharmed. We can make a clean exchange—evidence for people. No games, no tricks. Just a straightforward trade."

Carver was quiet for a moment. "And why would I believe you'd honor that deal? Why wouldn't you release the evidence anyway once your family is safe?"

"Because I'm not my father. He was an idealist who thought exposing you was worth dying for. I'm a realist who just wants his kids back." Atlas made his voice tired, defeated. "You've won, Carver. You've got all the leverage. I just want my family. Give them to me, and you can have your evidence. I don't care about justice or revenge anymore. I just want my children safe."

Another pause. Atlas could almost hear Carver thinking, weighing whether to believe him.

"You sound sincere, Mr. Drummond. Almost sincere enough to be believed." Carver's voice shifted, became harder. "But I didn't build an empire by trusting desperate men. So here's what's going to happen. The exchange will occur as planned, at the location and time I choose. You'll bring all the evidence—and I do mean all of it, every file, every copy, every backup. You'll bring the woman helping you, Ms. Brooks. And you'll both submit to a very thorough search to ensure you're not recording or transmitting."

"And my family?"

"Will be there. Alive and unharmed, assuming you cooperate fully. Make the exchange, prove the evidence is complete and all copies are destroyed, and everyone walks away. Betray me, and I'll kill them in front of you before I kill you. Do we understand each other?"

"Yes."

"Good. You'll receive the location in twenty-three hours. Be ready to move quickly—you'll have one hour to reach the site from when you receive the message. That should prevent you from having time to set up any surprises." Carver's voice took on an almost pleasant tone. "And Mr. Drummond? I respect that you're trying to save your family. It's admirable, really. Just don't mistake my respect for mercy. I've killed two hundred and thirty people in pursuit of my goals. I won't hesitate to kill six more if necessary."

The line went dead.

Atlas set down the phone, his hand steady despite the fear coursing through him.

"Did he buy it?" Hollis asked.

"I think so. But he's not stupid. He's going to be careful, paranoid. We'll only get one shot at this."

"Then we better make it count." Hollis pulled up a map on her laptop. "Twenty-three hours until we get the location. That gives us time to prepare, to get your team in position."

"We'll need to move fast once we get the location. He's giving us an hour to get there—not enough time to do a full recon, but enough to get people in place if we're smart." Atlas started making notes. "Rodriguez and the others—we'll brief them tonight at the warehouse. Give them communications equipment, weapons, assign sectors. When we get the location, they move into position while Hollis and I approach the exchange point."

"And when the shooting starts?"

"Then my team comes in hard and fast. We extract my family, neutralize the opposition, and get out." Atlas looked at Hollis. "But you won't be there. You'll be somewhere safe with the original evidence drives, ready to release everything if we don't make it."

"No." Hollis's voice was firm. "I'm coming with you. Carver specifically said I need to be there. If I'm not, it tips him off that something's wrong."

"Hollis—"

"Don't. We're partners, remember? I'm seeing this through." She closed her laptop. "Besides, you need me. I'm the only one who can verify the evidence is real, can navigate the files if Carver wants proof we're giving him everything. You can't do this without me."

She was right, and Atlas knew it. But the thought of bringing her into the exchange, into what would inevitably become a firefight, made his stomach clench.

"Okay," he said finally. "But you stay behind me at all times. You do exactly what I say, when I say it. Agreed?"

"Agreed."

Atlas checked his watch. 3:15 PM, Friday, October 24th. Just over thirty-four hours until the deadline. Twenty-three hours until they'd receive the location.

Everything came down to timing now. Preparation, positioning, and a whole lot of luck.

His phone—the new burner—buzzed. A text from Rodriguez: "Got three more guys interested. Seven total counting you. We good for 6 PM?"

Atlas texted back: "Good. Come ready to work. This is going to get messy."

The pieces were moving into place. Atlas had a team, had a plan—rough and incomplete, but better than nothing. In twenty-three hours, he'd know where the exchange would happen. And then it would be a race against time to save his family before Carver killed them all.

"We should eat something," Hollis said. "Can't fight on an empty stomach."

They ordered Chinese food delivery to the motel, ate in silence while reviewing files and making preparations. The food was tasteless, but Atlas forced it down. Hollis was right—they needed fuel.

At 5:30 PM, they left the motel and drove to Marcus's warehouse. Atlas took a deliberately complex route, watching for tails. Saw nothing, but couldn't shake the feeling they were being watched.

The warehouse was on the edge of the industrial district, a large corrugated metal building that Marcus used for his construction business. Tonight, it would serve as their operations center.

Rodriguez was already there when they arrived, along with Marcus and Davis. Three other men Atlas didn't recognize stood with them—clearly the additional recruits Rodriguez had mentioned.

"Ace." Rodriguez pulled Atlas into a brief hug. "Been too long, brother."

"Yeah, it has." Atlas looked at the assembled men. "Thanks for coming. All of you. This is going to be dangerous, possibly illegal, and you might end up dead or in prison. Anyone wants to walk away, now's the time."

Nobody moved.

"Alright then." Atlas pulled out his laptop, connected it to a large monitor Marcus had set up. "Here's the situation."

He spent the next hour briefing them. Explained about Project Genesis—carefully, not revealing everything, but enough that they understood what they were up against. Showed them photos of the opposition—Ashford, Carver, the private security forces they employed. Laid out what he knew about the exchange, which wasn't much.

"We're going in blind," Atlas admitted. "We won't know the location until tomorrow evening. We'll have one hour to get there and get in position. It's going to be rushed, chaotic, and a lot will depend on improvisation."

"So basically like every op we ever ran," Rodriguez said, getting a few chuckles from the others.

"Basically, yeah." Atlas pulled up tactical diagrams. "We'll split into three teams. Rodriguez, you'll command team one—three men, positioned to cover the primary approach. Marcus, you'll have team two—two men, covering the secondary approach. Davis, you're team three—solo, high ground if possible, overwatch with a long rifle."

Davis nodded. He'd been their designated marksman in Afghanistan.

"Hollis and I will make the actual exchange. The moment we confirm visual on my family, you move into position but hold fire. We'll try to make this work peacefully—get my family, hand over fake evidence, everyone walks away. But when it goes wrong, and it will go wrong, I'll give a code phrase over comms. That's your green light to engage."

"What's the code phrase?" one of the new guys asked.

"'The deal's done.'" Atlas met each man's eyes. "When you hear that, you come in hard. Priority one is extracting my family—my mother, my ex-wife, my two kids. Priority two is eliminating the hostiles. Priority three is Hollis and me. Clear?"

"Clear," they chorused.

"Equipment," Marcus said. "What do we need?"

"Communications—encrypted radios, everyone on the same channel. Body armor if you've got it. Weapons—whatever you're comfortable with, but bring plenty of ammunition. Medical supplies—at least one full trauma kit per team. Night vision if we have it."

"I've got NODs for everyone," Rodriguez said. "And body armor. Weapons won't be a problem."

They spent the next two hours going over details, running through scenarios, preparing equipment. It felt like old times, like getting ready for a mission in Afghanistan. Except this time it was personal.

At 8:30 PM, Atlas called a break. The men scattered to different parts of the warehouse—some checking weapons, some going over maps, some just sitting quietly in preparation for what was coming.

Hollis pulled Atlas aside. "They're good. Your team is really good."

"Best men I ever served with." Atlas watched Rodriguez methodically cleaning his rifle. "They'll do their jobs. Question is whether I've given them an impossible mission."

"We work with what we have. That's all anyone can do."

Atlas's old phone—still powered on from checking the earlier texts—buzzed with an email notification. He picked it up, expecting spam. Instead, he saw an address he didn't recognize: SafeHarbor2847@protonmail.co.

The subject line read: "Agent Morrison's Final Message."

Atlas opened it with shaking hands.

The message was short:

"Mr. Drummond - If you're reading this, I'm dead. I set up this automated email to send if I failed to check in for 24 hours. I was killed because I was getting too close to Project Genesis, and someone inside the FBI warned them.

I don't know who the mole is, but I know they're high-level. Trust no one in the Bureau. The only way to stop Project Genesis is to go public with everything.

I've attached my case files—everything I've compiled over two years. It's not as complete as what your father gathered, but it might help. Use it. Finish what we started.

And Mr. Drummond? Save your family first. Don't let them become more victims of this nightmare.

Rachel Morrison"

Atlas stared at the email, at this message from a dead woman who'd been trying to do the right thing. He clicked on the attachment—a large encrypted file that began downloading.

"What is it?" Hollis asked.

"Morrison. She set up a dead-man switch of her own." Atlas showed her the message. "She knew they might kill her. She made sure her evidence would survive even if she didn't."

"Then we use it. Add it to what your father compiled." Hollis took the phone, transferred the file to her laptop. "Between your father's evidence and Morrison's, we'll have everything we need to bury Project Genesis."

"After we save my family."

"After we save your family," Hollis agreed.

The warehouse door opened. A figure stepped inside—Torres, the fifth member of Atlas's original team. He'd said he needed time to think, but here he was.

"Sorry I'm late," Torres said, crossing to where Atlas stood. "Had to make sure my family was secure before I came. You know, in case this goes sideways and I don't make it back."

"You didn't have to come," Atlas said.

"Yeah, I did. You'd do the same for me." Torres looked around at the assembled team. "So where do you need me?"

Atlas felt a lump in his throat. These men—all of them—were risking everything to help him. Not for money, not for glory. Just because he'd asked.

"Team two," Atlas said. "With Marcus. You good with that?"

"Good with whatever you need, Ace."

They worked until midnight, finalizing plans, triple-checking equipment, making sure everyone knew their role. At 12:15 AM, Atlas called it.

"Get some sleep," he told them. "Be ready to move at a moment's notice starting at 5 PM tomorrow. We get the location at 6 PM, we roll out immediately. Questions?"

There were none.

The team dispersed. Rodriguez, Marcus, Davis, and Torres would stay at the warehouse, sleeping in shifts so someone was always watching the equipment. The three additional guys would go home but remain on standby.

Atlas and Hollis drove back to the motel. The city was quiet at this hour, most people asleep, unaware that tomorrow night would determine whether six people lived or died.

"You should try to sleep," Hollis said when they got back to the room. "Tomorrow's going to be brutal."

"So should you. You've been up for..." Atlas calculated. "Over forty hours now."

"I'll sleep after my 3 AM check-in." Hollis set an alarm on her phone. "Two more hours. I can make it two more hours."

Atlas lay down on one of the beds, still fully clothed, his gun within easy reach. Hollis sat at the table with her laptop, reviewing files, making final preparations.

"Hollis?"

"Yeah?"

"Thank you. For everything. For staying when you could have run. For risking your life for people you've never met."

Hollis turned to look at him. "Your kids aren't strangers to me. Not anymore. I've seen their pictures, heard you talk about them. They're real to me." She paused. "And besides, this stopped being just about your family the moment I found out my father was murdered. This is personal for both of us now."

"Still. Thank you."

"Thank me when everyone's safe and Project Genesis is exposed." Hollis turned back to her laptop. "Now sleep. I'll wake you if anything happens."

Atlas closed his eyes, but sleep was elusive. His mind kept running through scenarios, calculating odds, looking for the flaw in his plan that would get everyone killed.

Sometime after 2 AM, he must have dozed off, because he woke to Hollis shaking his shoulder.

"Check-in time," she said. "Just wanted you to know I'm doing it."

Atlas watched as she logged into the encrypted system, entered her passwords, confirmed her status. The screen updated: Next check-in required: 3:00 PM, Saturday, October 25th.

"Done," Hollis said. "If I miss that check-in, everything releases automatically. No going back."

"Good." Atlas sat up. "You should sleep now. I'll keep watch."

"Okay." Hollis lay down on the other bed, and within minutes she was asleep, exhaustion finally claiming her.

Atlas sat in the dark motel room, listening to Hollis breathe, checking his phones every few minutes, waiting for dawn.

Saturday, October 25th, 2025. The day his father's evidence would either save his family or get them all killed.

He had approximately eighteen hours until he'd receive the exchange location.

Eighteen hours to prepare for war.

Chapter 5: The Calm Before

Atlas woke to pale sunlight filtering through the motel curtains. For a moment, he didn't know where he was. Then it all came rushing back—his father dead, his family kidnapped, a billionaire holding their lives hostage.

He checked his phone. 9:47 AM, Saturday, October 25th.

Hollis was still asleep on the other bed, finally getting the rest she desperately needed. Atlas watched her for a moment, this woman who'd become his partner in the span of two days. She looked younger in sleep, vulnerable in a way she never allowed herself to be awake.

Atlas got up quietly, went to the bathroom, splashed water on his face. In the mirror, he barely recognized himself. Dark circles under his eyes, two days of stubble, the hollow look of someone running on fumes and desperation.

Less than nine hours until they'd receive the exchange location.

His burner phone sat on the nightstand, silent. No

new messages. The bad guys were waiting, confident in their control of the situation. They had all the leverage, or thought they did.

What they didn't know was that Atlas had a team. What they didn't know was that Hollis had set up dead-man switches that would expose everything if they failed. What they didn't know was that Atlas Drummond had been trained to fight in impossible situations, and he wasn't going down without taking as many of them with him as possible.

He made coffee using the motel's cheap machine, the smell gradually filling the small room. Hollis stirred, opened her eyes.

"What time is it?" she asked, her voice rough with sleep.

"Almost ten. You've been out for about seven hours."

"Seven hours?" Hollis sat up quickly. "Atlas, we should have—"

"Should have nothing. You needed rest. I kept watch. Everything's fine." Atlas handed her a cup of coffee. "How are you feeling?"

"Like I got hit by a truck." Hollis took the coffee

gratefully. "But better than I did yesterday. More human."

"Good. Because today's going to be worse than yesterday."

They sat in silence for a few minutes, both drinking coffee, both trying to prepare mentally for what was coming.

"I've been thinking," Hollis said finally. "About the exchange. About what happens after."

"After?"

"Assuming we survive. Assuming we get your family back and release all the evidence. What happens to us?" She looked at him. "We're going to be targets for the rest of our lives. Everyone connected to Project Genesis who escapes arrest will want us dead. We'll be looking over our shoulders forever."

Atlas had thought about this too. "Witness protection, maybe. New identities. Start over somewhere else."

"Would you do that? Leave your kids, never see them again?"

"To keep them safe? Yeah. I would." Atlas set down his coffee. "But I don't think it'll come to that. Once the evidence is public, once everyone knows what Project Genesis did, there's no point in killing us. The damage is done. Revenge wouldn't change anything."

"You really believe that?"

"I have to. Otherwise, what's the point of any of this?"

Hollis nodded slowly. "Okay. But Atlas—if things go wrong tonight, if we don't make it, I need you to know something."

"Don't. Don't do the goodbye speech. We're both making it out."

"Just let me say it." Hollis took a breath. "Meeting you was the best thing that could have come out of this nightmare. I know it's only been two days, but you've reminded me that there are still good people in the world. People worth fighting for."

Atlas felt something tighten in his chest. "Hollis—"

"I'm not done. If we make it through this, when we make it through this, I'd like to see where this goes. Us, I mean. Not just the investigation or the fighting, but... us."

Atlas looked at her, this fierce, brilliant woman who'd chosen to stand beside him when she could have run. "I'd like that too."

They held each other's gaze for a long moment. Then Hollis smiled, breaking the tension. "Okay. Now that I've made things awkward, what's the plan for today?"

"We wait. We prepare. At 6 PM, we get the location. Then we move." Atlas pulled out his laptop. "In the meantime, we should review Morrison's files. See if there's anything useful we missed."

They spent the next two hours going through the files Morrison's dead-man switch had sent. She'd been thorough—witness statements, financial records, surveillance photos. Her evidence corroborated everything Thomas Drummond had found and added new details.

"Look at this," Hollis said, pointing to a document. "Morrison identified three specific facilities in the US. One in Nevada, one in Georgia, one in upstate New York. These are the main research sites for Project Genesis."

Atlas studied the locations. "After tonight, assuming we survive, we need to make sure the FBI raids all of these simultaneously. If we take down Carver but leave the facilities operating, they'll just find new

leadership and continue."

"Already thought of that." Hollis pulled up a file she'd been working on. "I've prepared packages for the media and law enforcement. Everything organized, indexed, with executive summaries. The moment I trigger the release, every major news organization and federal agency will have everything they need to act immediately."

"You've been busy."

"I don't sleep much, remember?" Hollis smiled grimly. "Though I'm paying for it now. I feel like I could sleep for a week."

"After tonight, maybe you can."

Atlas's phone buzzed. Text from Rodriguez: "Team's ready. Waiting on your signal. Stay safe, brother."

Atlas texted back: "Six hours. Be ready to move."

"Your team's in position?" Hollis asked.

"Not yet. But they're ready. The moment we get the location, they'll mobilize." Atlas checked the time. 12:23 PM. "We should eat something. Real food, not just coffee."

They walked to a diner three blocks from the motel—not Pete's, somewhere new where they hadn't been seen before. Atlas kept scanning the street, looking for surveillance. Saw nothing obvious.

The diner was a family place, packed with the Saturday lunch crowd. Parents with kids, elderly couples, people living normal lives. Atlas watched a father cutting up pancakes for his young daughter and felt a physical ache. That should be him with Emma. That should be his normal Saturday.

Instead, he was preparing for what might be his last meal.

They ordered burgers and fries, ate mechanically. The food was good but Atlas barely tasted it. His mind was already at the exchange, running through scenarios.

"Stop," Hollis said quietly. "I can see you planning, calculating odds. Stop."

"I can't. Every decision I make tonight could mean the difference between my family living or dying."

"And you'll make better decisions if you're not exhausted and wound so tight you snap." Hollis reached across the table, took his hand. "Breathe. Just for a few minutes, let yourself breathe."

Atlas tried. Focused on the sensation of Hollis's hand in his, the ambient noise of the diner, the taste of coffee. Tried to be present instead of living in a future that hadn't happened yet.

It helped. A little.

They finished lunch and walked back to the motel. Atlas's phone showed 1:47 PM. Less than five hours until the location arrived.

Back in the room, Hollis set up her laptop. "I need to do my 3 PM check-in soon. After that, the next one would be 3 AM tomorrow. But we'll be in the middle of everything by then."

"So if you miss it, everything releases automatically."

"Exactly. Which means even if they kill us both during the exchange, the truth still gets out." Hollis pulled up the check-in screen. "It's our insurance policy."

"Our dead-man switch."

"Literally, yes."

At 3:00 PM exactly, Hollis completed her check-in. The screen updated: Next check-in required: 3:00 AM, Sunday, October 26th.

"Done," she said. "The countdown is running"If I don't check in twelve hours from now, everything goes public."

Atlas felt the weight of it. Twelve hours. In twelve hours, this would all be over, one way or another.

His phone rang. Unknown number, but not Carver's. Atlas answered cautiously.

"Mr. Drummond." The same voice from Thursday night—measured, controlled. "This is Victor Kozlov. We met briefly."

The man from the parking lot. The one who'd first threatened him.

"What do you want?"

"To give you some advice. Man to man, professional to professional." Kozlov's tone was almost friendly. "Don't try anything stupid tonight. Mr. Carver is prepared for every contingency. You bring the evidence, you get your family, everyone walks away. But if you try to be clever, if you have people waiting to ambush us, it will end badly for everyone you love."

"How do I know Carver will honor the deal?"

"You don't. But you know for certain what happens

if you don't show up or if you try to double-cross us. Your family dies. Painfully. Starting with the children." A pause. "I don't enjoy this work, Mr. Drummond. I don't like threatening children. But I'm very good at my job, and my job tonight is to ensure you cooperate. So please, for everyone's sake, cooperate."

"If anything happens to my kids—"

"Nothing will happen to them if you follow instructions. Six PM, you'll receive the location. One hour to arrive. Come with Ms. Brooks, bring all the evidence, submit to searches. Make the exchange and go home to your family. It's that simple."

The line went dead.

Atlas sat down heavily on the bed. "They know we're planning something. They're warning us off."

"Or they're just being cautious. Trying to psych us out." Hollis closed her laptop. "We stick to the plan. We don't have a choice."

"No. We don't."

The afternoon crawled by. Atlas tried to rest but couldn't. He cleaned his weapons, checked his equipment, went over maps and scenarios. Hollis organized files, strengthened encryption, made sure everything was ready for the automatic release if needed.

At 4:30 PM, Atlas called Rodriguez. "Status?"

"All teams ready. We're at the warehouse, geared up, waiting on your go. What's the ETA on the location?"

"Ninety minutes. The moment I have it, I'll send it to you. You'll have maybe forty-five minutes to get in position before Hollis and I arrive."

"Roger that. We'll be ready."

Atlas hung up and looked at Hollis. "Last chance to stay behind. To be somewhere safe."

"We've been through this. I'm coming." She pulled on her jacket. "Besides, Carver specifically said I need to be there. If I'm not, he'll know something's wrong."

"Okay. Then we both go in armed. They'll search us, but maybe we can hide something small. A backup weapon, a knife, something."

"Already thought of that." Hollis showed him a small folding knife, barely three inches. "Ceramic blade. Won't show up on metal detectors. I can hide it where they won't find it unless they strip-search me."

"And if they do strip-search you?"

"Then I'm unarmed and relying on your team to save us." Hollis's expression was grim. "Not ideal, but better than nothing."

Atlas checked his own backup options. A small .380 pistol in an ankle holster, easy to find if they searched carefully. A tactical pen—looks innocuous but could be used as a weapon. And a small knife similar to Hollis's, hidden where only an invasive search would find it.

Not much. But maybe enough to make a difference if things went bad.

5:30 PM. Thirty minutes until the location arrived.

Atlas and Hollis sat in the motel room, both silent, both preparing mentally for what was coming. The TV was on but muted, showing news coverage of Agent Morrison's murder. The FBI was calling it terrorism, promising a full investigation. They had no idea it was connected to Project Genesis.

Or maybe they did. Maybe Morrison's mole was already burying evidence, steering the investigation away from the truth.

It didn't matter. In a few hours, the truth would be public regardless of what the FBI did or didn't do.

5:45 PM. Fifteen minutes.

Atlas's hands were steady but his heart was pounding. This was it. The moment everything had been building toward. In fifteen minutes, he'd know where his family was being held. In less than two hours, he'd either have them back or watch them die.

"Whatever happens," Hollis said quietly, "we did everything we could."

"It won't be enough if they die."

"Then we make sure they don't die." Hollis stood up, checked her own weapons one more time. "We're good at this, Atlas. You're a trained soldier. I'm good with technology and I can handle myself in a fight. We have a team of professionals backing us up. The odds aren't as bad as they seem."

"The odds are terrible."

"Yeah. But we've got something they don't."

"What's that?"

"We're fighting for people we love. They're just following orders for money." Hollis met his eyes. "That matters. That makes us more dangerous than they expect."

5:55 PM. Five minutes.

Atlas pulled on body armor under his jacket. Hollis did the same. They looked at each other—two people about to walk into what was almost certainly a trap, knowing they might not walk back out.

"If we die tonight," Atlas said, "I want you to know I'm glad I met you. Glad you were with me for this."

"We're not dying tonight." Hollis's voice was firm. "We're going to save your family, expose Project Genesis, and then we're going to get very drunk and sleep for about twenty hours. That's the plan."

"I like that plan."

"Good. So let's make it happen."

6:00 PM exactly, Atlas's phone buzzed.

A text message. A location. And a map showing the route.

Atlas opened it, his hands surprisingly steady despite the adrenaline flooding his system.

The exchange point was forty-five minutes away. An abandoned industrial complex on the outskirts of the city. Multiple buildings, lots of cover, easy to defend and hard to assault.

Carver had chosen well.

Atlas immediately forwarded the location to Rodriguez. His phone rang seconds later.

"Got it," Rodriguez said. "We're rolling out now. We'll be in position in thirty-five minutes. That gives us ten minutes before you arrive to get set up."

"Make it count. This place is defensible. Lots of buildings, multiple angles of approach. They'll have overwatch, probably snipers."

"So will we. Davis is already plotting firing solutions. We'll have you covered."

"Good luck, brother."

"You too, Ace. Bring your family home."

Atlas hung up and looked at Hollis. "You ready?"

"As ready as I'll ever be."

They left the motel room for what might be the last time. Got in Atlas's truck, placed the bag containing the "evidence"—actually portable SSDs with dummy data, not the real files—on the back seat.

Atlas started the engine. Hollis pulled up the map on her phone, showing the route.

"Forty-five minutes," she said. "We should take it slow, make sure we're not followed. Get there right at the one-hour mark they gave us."

"Agreed."

They drove through the city as the sun began to set. Saturday evening, people heading out for dinner or movies, living normal lives. Atlas watched them through the windshield, these people who had no idea that somewhere on the edge of their city, a small war was about to begin.

He thought about Emma and Josh. Wondered if they were scared. Wondered if they understood what was happening or if they thought this was all some kind of mistake that Daddy would fix.

He was going to fix it. Whatever it took.

The city gave way to industrial areas, then to empty lots and abandoned buildings. The exchange location was in what used to be a manufacturing district, now just ruins and rust.

Atlas's phone buzzed. Text from Rodriguez: "In position. We have eyes on the site. Count at least 15 hostiles. They've got people on the roofs, vehicles positioned at exits. This is a serious setup."

Atlas texted back: "Copy. Stay hidden until my signal."

To Hollis, he said, "Fifteen guys. Plus however many are with my family. We're outnumbered at least two to one, maybe three to one."

"Then we better be smart." Hollis checked her weapons one last time. "The moment we confirm visual on your family, your team moves. We don't wait for them to start shooting. We strike first."

"Agreed."

They were five minutes from the location now. Atlas could see the complex ahead—a cluster of old warehouse buildings, dark against the darkening sky. Lights were visible in one of the central buildings. That's where they'd be. That's where his family was.

"Whatever happens in there," Atlas said, "stay close to me. If shooting starts, you get down and stay down until my team secures the area. Don't try to be a hero."

"Same to you." Hollis's voice was tight with tension. "Your kids need their father alive. Don't do anything stupid trying to save everyone at once."

"I'll try."

They pulled up to the entrance of the complex. A chain-link fence with an open gate. Two men standing guard, both armed with rifles, both watching Atlas's truck approach.

This was it. The point of no return.

Atlas drove through the gate, into the complex. Following hand signals from the guards, he navigated between buildings until he reached a large central courtyard.

Lights illuminated the space. At least a dozen armed men positioned around the perimeter. And in the center, standing beside a black SUV, was Edmund Carver himself.

He looked exactly like his photos—distinguished, patrician, but ravaged by cancer. Thin, pale, moving carefully like every step caused pain.

And beside the SUV, secured with plastic zip ties, were four people.

His mother. Sarah. Emma. Josh.

Atlas felt his heart clench. They were alive. They looked scared but unharmed.

Emma saw his truck and started crying. Josh tried

to run toward him but was yanked back by a guard.

"Easy," Hollis said quietly. "Stay calm. We confirm they're okay, we make the exchange, then we signal your team."

"Right." Atlas forced himself to breathe, to think tactically instead of emotionally. "Let's do this."

He stopped the truck in the center of the courtyard, about twenty feet from where Carver stood. Put it in park but left the engine running.

Both he and Hollis got out slowly, hands visible, making no sudden movements.

Carver smiled. "Mr. Drummond. Ms. Brooks. Thank you for being punctual. And for coming as requested." He gestured to the guards. "But before we proceed, my associates need to ensure you're not recording this encounter. Please submit to a search."

Two guards approached. Large men, professional in their movements. They patted down Atlas thoroughly, found his primary weapon, his backup pistol, the tactical pen. Took all of it.

One of them found the ankle holster and the small knife. "He's clean now."

They searched Hollis next. Found her primary weapon. One of them lingered on the search, hands moving places they didn't need to go. Hollis's expression was ice.

But they didn't find her ceramic knife. Didn't search thoroughly enough.

"She's clear," the guard finally said.

"Excellent." Carver stepped forward, moving carefully. "Now, the evidence. I trust you've brought everything?"

Atlas gestured to the truck. "Portable drives in the bag on the back seat. Everything my father compiled, everything Morrison had, all of it."

"Wonderful. Victor, please verify."

The man from Thursday night—Kozlov— walked to the truck, opened the back door, pulled out the bag. He examined the portable SSDs, connected one to a tablet computer, started scrolling through files.

This was the critical moment. The dummy data Hollis had prepared was good—real files, real names, enough to look legitimate on a quick check.

But if Kozlov dug deep enough, he'd realize something was wrong.

Atlas watched Kozlov's face. The man was scrolling, clicking, spot-checking files. Thirty seconds. A minute. Two minutes.

Finally, Kozlov nodded. "It's all here. Looks complete."

"Perfect." Carver smiled. "Then we have a deal, Mr. Drummond. Here's what happens next. You and Ms. Brooks will get in your truck and drive away. Once you're clear of the complex, my people will release your family. They'll be brought to a location I'll text you—somewhere public, safe. You'll be reunited within an hour. Everyone gets what they want."

"No." Atlas's voice was flat. "We take my family now. You keep the drives. We all leave together."

"That wasn't the deal."

"That's the new deal. You have what you want. Give me my family, and this ends."

Carver studied him. "You don't trust me to honor our agreement."

"Would you?"

A long pause. Then Carver laughed, a wheezing sound. "No. I suppose I wouldn't." He gestured to his

guards. "Release them. Let's conclude this business."

The guards cut the zip ties. Emma and Josh ran toward Atlas immediately. He caught them both, held them tight, felt their small bodies shaking against his.

"Daddy, we were so scared," Emma sobbed.

"I know, baby. I know. But it's over now. You're safe."

His mother and Sarah approached more slowly. His mother was crying. Sarah looked exhausted, traumatized, but alive.

"Everyone in the truck," Atlas said quietly. "Now."

He was guiding them toward the vehicle when Kozlov called out.

"Mr. Drummond. One more thing."

Atlas turned. Kozlov was still looking at the tablet, scrolling through files. His expression had changed.

"These files," Kozlov said slowly. "They're real. But they're not complete. There are folders here, but no contents. Placeholders." He looked up at Carver. "Sir, I think these are decoys."

Everything stopped.

Carver's expression went from satisfied to furious in an instant. "You tried to deceive me?"

"No," Atlas said, his hand moving to where his weapon should have been and finding nothing. "That's everything we have."

"Liar!" Carver's voice was a shout despite his weakened state. "You gave me fake evidence!"

"The evidence is real. Check any file you want —"

"The critical files are missing. The financial records, the top-level connections. You gave me enough to verify it's real but held back the most damaging information." Carver's face was twisted with rage. "Did you really think I wouldn't notice?"

Atlas's mind raced. The dummy data should have been perfect. Hollis had spent hours—

Then he saw it. Hollis's expression. Not shocked. Not scared. Resigned.

She'd sabotaged the dummy data. Made it good enough to pass a quick check but not deep scrutiny. She'd ensured that even if they failed, even if Atlas tried to make a real deal with Carver, the exchange wouldn't work.

She'd forced them into the fight Atlas had been trying to avoid.

"Hollis," Atlas said quietly. "What did you do?"

"What I had to." Hollis's voice was steady. "I'm sorry, Atlas. But I couldn't let you trade the real evidence. Couldn't let these people get away with murder. Even for your family."

Atlas felt everything collapsing. The plan was ruined. They were surrounded by armed men. His family was here, in the line of fire.

Carver pulled out a gun—a small pistol that looked huge in his wasted hands. Pointed it at Josh.

"Then I'm afraid we have a problem, Mr. Drummond."

Atlas saw it happening in slow motion. Carver's finger tightening on the trigger. Josh's eyes going wide with terror. Emma screaming.

Atlas moved. Threw himself between Carver and his son.

And spoke the code phrase into the microphone hidden in his jacket collar.

"The deal's done."

Then the world exploded into chaos.

Chapter 6: Chaos And Fire

The first shot came from Davis.

Atlas heard it even as he was moving—the sharp crack of a high-powered rifle from somewhere in the darkness beyond the courtyard lights. One of Carver's rooftop snipers dropped.

Then Rodriguez and his team opened up from three different positions simultaneously.

Gunfire erupted from every direction. Carver's men scattered, looking for cover, returning fire toward muzzle flashes they could barely see. The courtyard, carefully lit and controlled moments before, became a chaotic battlefield.

Atlas grabbed Josh with one arm, Emma with the other, and threw himself behind his truck. "Get down! Stay down!"

Sarah and his mother were right behind him, both screaming. Bullets pinged off metal, shattered windows, tore through the truck's body panels.

Hollis had her ceramic knife out and was cutting the zip ties still dangling from Sarah's wrists. "Stay behind the truck! Don't move unless Atlas tells you to!"

Atlas risked a look around the front bumper. Carver had taken cover behind the SUV, his guards forming a protective shield around him. Kozlov was shouting orders, directing his men to return fire.

At least three of Carver's guards were down already. Rodriguez's team had the advantage of surprise and superior positioning. But there were still too many hostiles, and Atlas's family was caught in the middle.

"We need to move!" Atlas shouted to Hollis over the gunfire. "Get them to that building!" He pointed to a warehouse structure about thirty yards away. Closer cover, better protection than the truck which was rapidly being shot to pieces.

"On three!" Hollis shouted back.

"One... two... THREE!"

They moved as a group, Atlas leading with Emma in his arms, Hollis bringing up the rear with Josh. Sarah and his mother ran between them, bent low.

Bullets kicked up dirt around their feet. A round passed so close to Atlas's head he felt the displacement of air. But they made it, throwing themselves through an open doorway into the darkness of the warehouse.

"Stay here!" Atlas ordered. "Don't move, don't make a sound!"

"Atlas, no!" His mother grabbed his arm. "Don't go back out there!"

"I have to. My team is out there fighting. I'm not letting them do this alone." Atlas kissed her forehead, then Emma's, then Josh's. "I love you. All of you. I'll be back."

He turned to Hollis. "You're armed. You protect them. Anyone comes through that door who isn't me or my team, you put them down. Understand?"

Hollis pulled out her ceramic knife. It looked pathetically small. "I need a gun, Atlas."

"I know. Working on it." Atlas looked back toward the courtyard. The firefight was still raging. "Stay here. I mean it."

He slipped back out into the chaos.

The courtyard was a nightmare of muzzle flashes and ricochets. Atlas stayed low, moving from cover to cover, working his way toward where one of Carver's guards had fallen. The man was dead, but he had a rifle—an AR-15 variant with a half-empty magazine.

Atlas grabbed it, checked the chamber, did a quick

press check. Good to go.

His radio crackled. Rodriguez's voice: "Ace, where are you? What's your status?"

Atlas keyed the mic. "Family's secure in building three. I'm mobile. What's the situation?"

"We've got them pinned but they're not breaking. They've got at least two guys with squad automatics laying down serious fire. We can't advance without taking casualties."

"Where's Davis?"

"Rooftop, north side. He's taken out three of their snipers but there's at least one more he can't get an angle on."

Atlas scanned the battlefield, his military training kicking in. He could see the problem—Carver's men had good cover and overlapping fields of fire. Rodriguez's team was winning on firepower but couldn't close the distance.

They needed something to break the stalemate.

Atlas saw it—a vehicle, one of Carver's SUVs, positioned near the center of the courtyard. If he could get to it, start it, use it as a battering ram or mobile

cover...

"Cover me," Atlas said into the radio. "I'm going for the vehicle."

"Negative, that's suicide—"

But Atlas was already moving.

He sprinted across fifteen yards of open ground, bullets chasing him, and threw himself into a slide behind a concrete barrier. Breathed for two seconds, then moved again. Another sprint, this time to a pile of crates.

The SUV was ten yards away.

Atlas took a breath, said a prayer, and ran.

Bullets tore through the air around him. He felt one tug at his jacket, another burn across his thigh—a graze, painful but not disabling. Then he was at the SUV, yanking open the door, throwing himself inside.

Keys in the ignition. These people were professionals but they'd gotten overconfident. Thought they had total control.

Atlas started the engine and slammed it into drive.

He roared across the courtyard directly at Carver's position, the SUV's engine screaming. Men scattered. Someone fired a burst that shattered the windshield, and Atlas ducked low, driving blind, just trying to create chaos.

The SUV slammed into something—another vehicle, maybe a barrier—and Atlas was thrown forward, his head cracking against the steering wheel despite the seatbelt.

Stars exploded across his vision. He shook his head, trying to clear it, and realized the SUV had stopped directly between Carver's position and where Rodriguez's team was firing from.

He'd accidentally created cover for both sides.

Atlas kicked open the door and rolled out, still clutching the rifle. His head was ringing, blood running down his face from a cut on his forehead.

"Alpha team, advance!" Rodriguez's voice over the radio. "We've got cover now!"

Atlas heard boots pounding across concrete. Rodriguez and his team were moving up, using the SUV as mobile cover just like Atlas had planned—except he'd planned to be driving it, not crashed into it.

Gunfire intensified as the distance closed. Close quarters now, almost hand-to-hand range.

Atlas saw Kozlov emerge from cover, assault rifle up and firing. Atlas brought up his own weapon and fired a three-round burst. Kozlov went down hard.

More of Carver's men were falling. The tide was turning.

Then Atlas saw him—Edmund Carver himself, being dragged toward a vehicle at the far end of the courtyard by two remaining guards. They were trying to escape.

"Rodriguez, Carver's running! East side!"

"I see him! Davis, do you have a shot?"

Davis's voice came over the radio: "Negative, too much smoke and interference. He's in dead space from my angle."

Atlas started running. His leg burned where the bullet had grazed him, and his head was still spinning from hitting the steering wheel, but he pushed through it. Carver was not getting away.

One of the guards saw Atlas coming and turned to engage. They both fired at the same time. Atlas felt something punch into his body armor—right over his ribs, painful but not penetrating. His own burst caught the guard center mass and the man went down.

The second guard was faster, more skilled. He got behind cover and returned fire, forcing Atlas to dive behind a concrete pillar.

They traded shots, neither getting an advantage.

Then Marcus appeared from a flanking position and put two rounds into the guard's back. The man fell.

"Carver's at the vehicle!" Atlas shouted.

But they were too late. Carver's driver—someone they'd missed in the initial assault—got him into the back seat and the vehicle was moving, tires squealing as it accelerated toward an exit.

Davis's rifle cracked once. The vehicle swerved but kept going. Either he'd missed or it wasn't enough to stop them.

"Let him go," Rodriguez said, appearing beside Atlas. "We got your family. That was the mission."

"We can't let him escape—"

"Look around, Ace." Rodriguez gestured at the courtyard. "We've got wounded. We've got your mom and kids traumatized and needing medical attention. We've got dead bodies and enough evidence of a firefight to bring every cop in the city down on us. We need to extract and disappear, right now."

Atlas wanted to argue. Wanted to chase Carver down and finish this. But Rodriguez was right. The mission was to save his family, and they'd done that.

"Fine. Get everyone mobile. We're leaving in two minutes."

The next two minutes were chaos of a different kind. Torres appeared with a truck he'd "requisitioned"—stolen—from somewhere. Marcus and another contractor were helping wounded move. Davis came down from his overwatch position, his rifle still smoking.

Atlas ran back to the warehouse where he'd left his family. Burst through the door to find Hollis standing guard, knife in hand, his mother and ex-wife huddled in a corner with Emma and Josh pressed between them.

"It's me! It's over! We need to move!"

Emma and Josh ran to him. He scooped them both up despite his injuries, carried them outside. Hollis helped his mother and Sarah.

The courtyard looked like a war zone. Bodies everywhere, vehicles shot to pieces, brass casings and blood on the concrete. At least eight of Carver's men dead, maybe more.

Atlas's team had taken casualties too. One of the contractors he didn't know well was being carried by Rodriguez, blood soaking through his jacket. Another was limping badly, his leg bandaged with field dressings.

"Into the truck!" Rodriguez was directing traffic, getting everyone loaded. "We've got maybe five minutes before cops start showing up. Move, people!"

Atlas got his family into Torres's truck, then helped load the wounded. His own injuries were superficial compared to some—the grazing wound on his leg, the cut on his head, bruised ribs from the bullet that hit his armor.

"Sir!" One of the contractors, a young guy named Miller, was pointing at something. "The bag with the evidence drives! It's still in Mr. Drummond's truck!"

Atlas looked. His truck was a wreck, windows shot out, body panels destroyed. But the bag was visible in the back seat.

"Leave it," Atlas said. "Those are dummy drives anyway."

"But if the cops find them—"

"Let them. Let them find evidence of Project Genesis. Let them investigate." Atlas climbed into Torres's truck. "We've got what we came for. Everything else is secondary."

Rodriguez did a final headcount, confirmed everyone was accounted for, then gave the signal. Three vehicles—Torres's truck, Rodriguez's SUV, and Marcus's van—pulled out of the complex, leaving the carnage behind.

They split up immediately, each vehicle taking a different route. Atlas's family was with him in Torres's truck, along with Hollis and Torres himself driving. They headed east while the others went north and south.

In the back seat, Emma was crying softly. Josh had gone silent, traumatized into muteness. Sarah held them both, her face pale with shock. Atlas's mother sat beside him in the front, her hand gripping his so tight it hurt.

"Is it over?" his mother asked. "Is it really over?"

"Not yet," Atlas said honestly. "But the worst part is. You're safe now. All of you."

Torres drove carefully, not too fast, obeying all traffic laws. They couldn't afford to get pulled over. Not covered in blood and gun residue, not with traumatized children in the back.

Hollis's phone buzzed. She checked it, her expression tightening. "News alert. Reports of a shooting at an industrial complex. Multiple casualties. Police are responding."

"How long do you think we have before they ID everyone?" Torres asked.

"Depends how thorough Carver's people were about covering their tracks," Atlas said. "Could be hours. Could be minutes. We need to assume the worst."

"Where are we going?"

Good question. They couldn't go back to the motel—too obvious. Couldn't go to any of their homes—first place the cops would look if they connected any of this to Project Genesis.

"We need to split up," Atlas decided. "Hollis, you take the evidence to the safest place you can think of. Trigger the release protocol. Get everything public before anyone can stop us."

"What about you?"

"I'm taking my family somewhere safe. Somewhere off-grid where we can hide while this blows over."

"Atlas, if you run, you'll look guilty—"

"I am guilty. We all are. We just conducted an armed assault that left at least eight people dead." Atlas looked at his children, still shaking with fear. "But I'm not letting my kids anywhere near an interrogation room or a trial. Not after what they've been through."

Hollis was quiet for a moment. Then she nodded. "Okay. Where do you want me to drop you?"

"Anywhere we can get another vehicle. Someplace with a lot of cars, lots of people. A mall, maybe."

Torres drove to a large shopping mall on the outskirts of the city. Saturday night, the parking lot was packed. Torres pulled into a space near the back, away from security cameras.

"This is where we part ways," Atlas said. "Torres, you should ditch this truck and disappear for a while. Take the wounded contractors to a doctor who doesn't ask questions, then lay low."

"What about payment? We did the job—"

"Check your account in twenty-four hours. I'll make sure everyone gets what they're owed." Atlas opened the door, helped his family out. "And Torres? Thank you. You saved lives tonight."

Torres nodded. "Take care of those kids, Ace. That's payment enough."

Atlas turned to Hollis. She stood in the parking lot, this woman he'd known for less than three days, who'd become the most important person in his world aside from his family.

"Release the evidence," he said. "All of it. Everything my father found, everything Morrison compiled, all the connections to Carver and Helix Innovations. Burn it all down."

"I will." Hollis stepped close, put her hand on his cheek. "And when this is over, when the dust settles, find me. Don't disappear forever."

"I won't. I promise."

They kissed, brief but fierce. Then Hollis got back in the truck with Torres and they drove away, leaving Atlas standing in a parking lot with his traumatized family and no clear plan for what came next.

"Daddy, where are we going?" Emma asked in a small voice.

"Somewhere safe, baby. Somewhere no one will find us."

He led them through the mall, looking for a target. Found it in the parking structure—a older model SUV, something without modern anti-theft systems. Atlas had learned how to hotwire vehicles in the Army. It took him three minutes to get the SUV started.

"We're stealing a car?" Sarah asked, her voice shocked.

"Borrowing. I'll make sure the owner is compensated." Atlas got everyone loaded. "Right now, staying mobile is more important than staying legal."

He drove north, away from the city, heading toward rural areas where law enforcement was sparse and people didn't ask too many questions. They needed a place to hide for at least twenty-four hours while Hollis released the evidence and the story broke.

After that, everything would change. Project Genesis would be exposed. The deaths, the experiments, Carver's involvement—all of it public. And hopefully, in the chaos and media frenzy, Atlas and his family could slip through the cracks and disappear.

His phone buzzed. Text from Hollis: "Evidence release initiated. Every major news outlet and federal agency will have everything in approximately 15 minutes. It's done, Atlas. Your father's investigation, Morrison's work, all of it is about to go public. Whatever happens now, we won."

Atlas felt something release in his chest. Relief, maybe. Or just exhaustion.

They'd done it. The truth was coming out. Project Genesis would be exposed, destroyed, all its victims finally acknowledged.

His father hadn't died for nothing.

"Atlas, your leg is bleeding," his mother said, noticing the wound for the first time.

"It's just a graze. I'm fine."

"You're not fine. None of us are fine." Sarah's voice was strained. "We were kidnapped, held hostage, nearly killed. The kids watched people die. We heard gunfire, saw violence—God, Atlas, what have we been through?"

"I know. I know it was horrible." Atlas glanced in the rearview mirror at his children. Emma was crying silently. Josh was still staring at nothing, his eyes unfocused. "But you're alive. That's what matters. You're alive and safe and we're together."

"For how long? Until the police catch up with us? Until whoever's left from Project Genesis comes after us for revenge?"

"That's not going to happen. The evidence is public

now. There's no point in coming after us—the damage is done."

"You don't know that."

"No. But I believe it." Atlas reached over and took his mother's hand. "And right now, belief is all we've got."

They drove for two more hours, finally stopping at a small motel in a rural town whose name Atlas didn't even catch. He paid cash, gave a fake name, took two adjoining rooms.

Once inside, he turned on the TV. Every news channel was already covering it. The story was breaking everywhere simultaneously, exactly as Hollis had planned.

"Breaking news tonight: massive scandal involving illegal human experiments by biotech company Helix Innovations. Documents released to news organizations show evidence of hundreds of deaths, conspiracy at the highest levels..."

Atlas watched for a few minutes, then turned it off. He'd hear the rest later. Right now, his family needed him.

Emma and Josh were sitting on one of the beds, still silent and scared. Atlas sat between them, pulled

them close.

"I know what you saw tonight was scary," he said quietly. "I know you don't understand what's happening. But I promise you, the bad people who took you are gone now. They can't hurt you anymore."

"Are we going to jail?" Josh asked in a whisper.

"No, buddy. We're not going to jail."

"But we were in a fight. People got hurt."

"I know. But that wasn't your fault. None of this was your fault." Atlas kissed the top of Josh's head. "The people who did bad things are going to be punished. But you're safe. You're with me, and I will never let anyone hurt you."

Emma looked up at him with red-rimmed eyes. "Did you kill people, Daddy?"

Atlas closed his eyes. He'd hoped to avoid this question, at least for tonight. But Emma was too smart, had seen too much.

"Yes," he said honestly. "I did. To protect you. To save you and your brother and grandma and mom."

"Does that make you a bad person?"

"I don't know, sweetheart. That's something I'm going to have to live with. But I'd do it again in a heartbeat if it meant keeping you safe."

Emma thought about this, then snuggled closer to him. "I'm glad you saved us, Daddy."

"Me too, baby. Me too."

In the other room, Atlas could hear his mother and Sarah talking in low voices. Probably trying to process what had happened, trying to figure out what came next.

Atlas had no answers for them. He'd saved them tonight, but he'd also destroyed his life in the process. He was a fugitive now, wanted for questioning at minimum, possibly for murder depending on how the investigation went.

His career was over. His normal life was over. Everything he'd built since leaving the Army—gone.

But his family was alive. And that was worth everything.

His phone buzzed. Text from Rodriguez: "All teams accounted for. Two wounded, both stable. We're going dark for a while. Take care of yourself, brother. You did good tonight."

Another text, this one from Hollis: "Evidence is everywhere. Front page of every major site, trending on social media, federal agencies scrambling to respond. We did it, Atlas. Project Genesis is finished."

Atlas set down his phone and held his children close, listening to them breathe, feeling their heartbeats against his chest.

They'd won. They'd survived.

Now they just had to figure out how to live with what they'd done.

Chapter 7: Fallout

Atlas woke to the sound of his phone ringing. For a moment, he didn't know where he was. Then it all came back—the motel, the escape, his family sleeping in the adjoining room.

He grabbed the phone. 6:47 AM, Sunday, October 26th. Unknown number.

He answered. "Hello?"

"Mr. Drummond," a woman's voice said, professional and authoritative. "This is Assistant Director Patricia Moss, FBI. We need to talk."

Atlas sat up, instantly alert. "How did you get this number?"

"The same way we tracked your location to within a five-mile radius. The same way we know you were at that industrial complex last night," Moss replied. "But that's not why I'm calling. I'm calling because I need to know if you have more evidence beyond what was released last night."

"Why would I tell you that?" Atlas asked.

"Because right now, the entire federal law

enforcement apparatus is mobilizing to shut down Project Genesis. We have teams preparing to raid facilities in Nevada, Georgia, and New York. We have warrants being drafted for Edmund Carver, Dr. Lawrence Ashford, and at least forty other individuals." Moss paused. "But if there's additional evidence we don't have, evidence that could help us build stronger cases or identify more facilities, I need it now."

Atlas thought about Morrison's files, still on Hollis's laptop. The financial records his father had compiled that weren't in the public release. The connections to other billionaires who might have funded Project Genesis.

"There might be more," Atlas said carefully. "But I need something in return."

"I'm listening," Moss said.

"Immunity. For me, for everyone who helped me last night. We walk away from the firefight, no charges, no prosecution."

"That's not my call—"

"Then get someone on the phone who can make that call," Atlas interrupted. "Because in about three minutes, I'm hanging up and disappearing. You'll never

find me, and you'll never get the additional evidence."

Moss was quiet. Atlas could hear voices in the background, people conferring. Then she said, "Hold on."

A minute passed. Then a new voice came on the line—male, older, with the gravelly tone of someone who'd spent a lifetime in law enforcement.

"Mr. Drummond, this is Director James Walsh, FBI," the man said. "Director Moss tells me you're demanding immunity in exchange for additional evidence."

"That's right," Atlas confirmed.

"I can't give you blanket immunity. Eight people died last night. There has to be an accounting."

"Those eight people were holding my family hostage," Atlas said. "They were part of an organization that murdered over two hundred people. They got what they deserved."

"Maybe. But that's for a court to decide, not you," Walsh replied. His voice softened slightly. "However, I can offer you this: cooperate fully, provide all evidence, testify in the trials that are coming, and I'll personally ensure the Justice Department considers it a justified action. Self-defense, defense of family. You'll face questioning, possibly a grand jury, but I'll fight to keep you and your team out of prison."

"That's not good enough," Atlas said.

"It's the best you're going to get. And frankly, Mr. Drummond, it's better than you deserve. You conducted a military assault on U.S. soil. You killed people, regardless of how justified you think it was. The law still applies." Walsh paused. "Your father died trying to expose these people. Agent Morrison died trying to stop them. Don't let their sacrifices be wasted because you're too proud to accept help."

The line went dead.

Atlas sat on the edge of the bed, head in his hands. Everything had seemed so clear last night— save his family, expose Project Genesis, let the chips fall where they may. But now, in the cold light of morning, the consequences were becoming real.

He was a fugitive. His team members were fugitives. They'd killed people, regardless of justification. And the federal government wanted him to turn himself in.

A knock on the connecting door interrupted his thoughts. His mother's voice came through: "Atlas? Are

you awake?"

"Yeah, Mom. Come in," Atlas called back.

She entered, looking exhausted. "The kids are still asleep. Sarah too. But I've been watching the news." She sat beside him on the bed. "It's everywhere. Project Genesis, the experiments, Edmund Carver. They're calling it the biggest biotech scandal in history."

"Good. That's what we wanted," Atlas said.

"The news is covering the firefight. Eight dead, multiple wounded. They're calling it 'under investigation.'" His mother looked at him with worry. "Are they going to connect this to you? To what you did to save us?"

"Yeah. The FBI already called. They know," Atlas admitted.

"Oh, Atlas." She took his hand. "What's going to happen to you now?"

"I don't know. But I did what I had to do to save you. To save the kids." Atlas met her eyes. "And I'd do it again. Every single bit of it."

"But now what? What did they say?" his mother asked.

"They're giving me two hours to decide whether to cooperate or run," Atlas explained.

"What are you going to do?"

"I don't know." Atlas stood up, started pacing. "If I cooperate, I might avoid prison. Might. But I'll put everyone through years of legal hell. Grand juries, trials, testimony. The kids will have to relive everything that happened."

"And if you run?" his mother asked.

"We disappear. New identities, new lives. But we'll always be looking over our shoulders. And I'll never be able to use my real name, see my friends, live a normal life again."

His mother was quiet for a long moment. Then she asked, "What would your father do?"

Atlas thought about Thomas Drummond. About his obsessive need for justice, his belief in doing the right thing regardless of personal cost.

"He'd cooperate. He'd testify, help build the cases, make sure everyone involved in Project Genesis faced justice." Atlas sat back down. "He'd do the right thing even if it destroyed him."

"Your father wasn't always right about everything," his mother said. "Sometimes doing the right thing for strangers means doing the wrong thing for your family."

"But if I run, if I hide, doesn't that make me just like them? Like Carver and Ashford, using my resources to escape consequences?"

"No. Because you're not running from justice. You're protecting your children from further trauma." His mother squeezed his hand. "Atlas, I love you. I'm proud of what you did last night. But those children in the next room need their father more than the FBI needs another witness. If you need to run, if that's what keeps this family together, then run. I'll support you."

Before Atlas could respond, his phone rang again. Different number. He answered.

"Atlas, it's Hollis," she said.

Relief flooded through him. "Are you okay? Where are you?"

"Safe. Can't say where over the phone," Hollis replied. "But I wanted you to know—the evidence release worked even better than we hoped. Every major news organization is running it. The FBI has already started executing search warrants. Three facilities raided in the

last two hours, over fifty people arrested."

"That's good. That's what we wanted," Atlas said.

"But there's something else. Something I found in Morrison's files that wasn't in the public release." Hollis's voice dropped. "Atlas, Edmund Carver isn't the only billionaire involved in Project Genesis. There are at least three others—major players in biotech and pharmaceuticals. Morrison had identified them but didn't have enough evidence to prove their involvement."

"So there are more people out there, more funding?" Atlas asked.

"Exactly. Project Genesis is bigger than just Carver. Even with him on the run and Helix Innovations being shut down, the other investors could restart the operation somewhere else. Different name, different front company, same horrific experiments," Hollis explained.

Atlas felt a chill. They'd cut off one head of the hydra, but others remained.

"What do we do?" he asked.

"We finish what your father started. We identify all the investors, expose all the connections, make sure every single person involved goes down." Hollis paused. "But I can't do it alone. I need you. I need your father's files, the financial records, everything we held back from the public release."

"Hollis, the FBI just called me. They want me to cooperate, testify, hand over all remaining evidence. If I don't, they'll hunt me as a fugitive," Atlas said.

"Then cooperate. Give them what they need to finish this," Hollis urged.

"And go to prison?"

"You won't go to prison. Not for saving your family. Not when the alternative was letting Carver's people kill you all." Hollis's voice was fierce. "Atlas, you're a hero. You exposed one of the worst criminal conspiracies in modern history. The FBI knows that. The public knows that. You'll be fine."

"You sound very certain," Atlas said.

"I am certain. Because I've already been contacted by three different lawyers offering to represent you pro bono. Because there are petitions online with hundreds of thousands of signatures supporting you. Because people understand you did what you had to do." Hollis softened her tone. "Come in from the cold, Atlas. Let's finish this together. The right way."

Atlas looked at the connecting door, behind which

his family was sleeping. Thought about Emma and Josh, about the life they deserved to have. Normal, safe, free from fear.

Could they have that life if he was testifying in trials for the next several years? Could they have it if they were living under fake names in hiding?

Maybe neither option was good. Maybe they were both terrible in different ways.

But one option involved facing the consequences of his actions. Taking responsibility, helping ensure justice was done. Living with integrity even if it was hard.

The other option involved running, hiding, teaching his children that when things got difficult, you disappeared rather than faced them.

"Okay," Atlas said. "I'll cooperate. But Hollis, I need you to do something for me first."

"Anything," she replied.

"The remaining evidence—the financial records, the connections to other investors. Make copies. Multiple copies in multiple locations. Because if something happens to me, if the FBI doesn't follow through or if someone tries to bury this, I need to know the truth will still come out."

"Already done," Hollis assured him. "I've got dead-man switches set up for the additional evidence, separate from the first release. If anything happens to either of us, everything goes public automatically."

"Good. That's good." Atlas checked the time. He had ninety minutes left on Walsh's deadline. "I need to talk to my family first. Explain what's happening. Then I'll call Walsh back and arrange to turn myself in."

"Atlas?" Hollis said.

"Yeah?"

"You're doing the right thing. Your father would be proud."

After they hung up, Atlas sat for a few more minutes, gathering his courage. Then he went to the connecting door and knocked softly.

Sarah answered, looking haggard. Behind her, Emma and Josh were awake, sitting on the bed and watching cartoons on the TV.

"We need to talk," Atlas said. "All of us."

Ten minutes later, they were all gathered in one room—Atlas, his mother, Sarah, Emma, and Josh. Atlas explained the situation as simply as he could. The FBI wanted him to cooperate. He would have to answer questions, possibly testify in trials. There might be legal consequences, though hopefully nothing serious.

"Does this mean we're going home?" Josh asked.

"Eventually. First, we'll probably stay in a safe location while the FBI wraps up their investigation. But yes, you'll get to go home," Atlas told him.

"To our real home? With my room and my toys?" Josh pressed.

Atlas looked at Sarah. She nodded slightly. "Yes, buddy. Your real home," he confirmed.

Emma was quieter, more thoughtful. "Daddy, will you have to go to jail?"

"I hope not, sweetheart. But I might have to go away for a while to answer questions and help the good guys catch the bad guys," Atlas explained.

"But you'll come back?" Emma asked.

"I'll always come back to you. I promise," Atlas said.

Sarah spoke up. "Atlas, are you sure about this? Turning yourself in?"

"No. But it's the right thing to do." He looked at his ex-wife. "I'm sorry. For all of this. For dragging you into my mess, for putting the kids in danger."

"You didn't drag us in. They took us to get to you," Sarah said. Her expression was complex— anger, fear, but also something that might have been understanding. "You saved us. I haven't forgotten that."

"Still. If I'd been smarter, more careful—"

"Then your father's killers would have gotten away with it. Project Genesis would still be operating. More people would die." Sarah shook her head. "I don't like what happened. I'm terrified of what comes next. But I understand why you did it."

Atlas called Director Walsh at exactly 8:47 AM.

"I'll cooperate," he said. "Full cooperation. All evidence, all testimony, whatever you need."

"Smart choice, Mr. Drummond," Walsh replied. "Where are you?"

Atlas gave him the location of the motel. "But my family needs protection. Safe housing, security. I'm not letting them be exposed while we work through this."

"Agreed. I'm dispatching agents now. They'll be

there in approximately ninety minutes. In the meantime, stay where you are, don't talk to anyone, and don't destroy any evidence," Walsh instructed.

"One more thing. The people who helped me last night—my team. They get immunity too. Full immunity, no exceptions," Atlas said.

"I can't promise—" Walsh began.

"Then we don't have a deal. Those men risked their lives to save my family. They're not going to prison for doing the right thing," Atlas insisted.

Walsh was quiet for a moment. Then he said, "I'll do what I can. No promises, but I'll make the case for immunity. That's the best I can offer."

It would have to be enough.

The next ninety minutes were tense. Atlas watched the parking lot, waiting for FBI vehicles to arrive, half-expecting Carver's remaining people to show up instead for one final attempt at revenge.

But nothing happened. Just an ordinary Sunday morning at a rural motel. Families loading luggage into cars, kids running around the parking lot, people living normal lives.

At 10:15 AM, three black SUVs pulled into the parking lot. Professional, coordinated, unmistakably federal agents.

"They're here," Atlas announced.

His mother hugged him. Sarah hugged him. Emma and Josh clung to him, not wanting to let go.

"It's okay," Atlas told them. "These are the good guys. They're going to help us."

The agents were polite, professional. They took Atlas into custody—technically not under arrest, just "protective custody pending questioning"—and separately secured his family. Different vehicles, different destinations. Protocol, they said. Standard procedure.

Atlas was driven to a federal building in the nearest major city, taken to an interview room, and left alone for twenty minutes. Standard intimidation tactic. Let the suspect sweat, wonder what's coming.

But Atlas had been through worse. Twenty minutes was nothing.

Finally, Director Walsh and Assistant Director Moss entered. They sat across from him, pulled out recording devices, and began.

"Let's start at the beginning," Walsh said. "Tell us everything."

So Atlas did. He told them about his father's investigation, about meeting Hollis at McGinty's Bar, about finding the evidence in the storage unit. He told them about Carver's threats, about his mother and family being kidnapped, about the impossible choice he'd faced.

He told them about recruiting his team, about planning the assault, about the firefight that left eight of Carver's people dead.

He held nothing back. Every detail, every decision, every bullet fired.

The interview lasted six hours. They took breaks, brought him water and food, collected the remaining evidence drives from his possession, but kept pressing for details. Walsh and Moss were relentless but not cruel. They were building a case—not against Atlas, but against Project Genesis. They needed his testimony to be ironclad.

Finally, at 4:30 PM, they stopped the recording.

"That's enough for today," Walsh announced. "We'll need more sessions, but we've got the framework."

"What happens now?" Atlas asked.

"Now we process everything you've told us, cross-reference it with the evidence you provided, and continue building cases against everyone involved in Project Genesis." Walsh leaned back.

"You did good work, Mr. Drummond. Your father would be proud."

"What about my team? The men who helped me?" Atlas pressed.

"Still working on it. The Justice Department is... resistant to granting immunity for a firefight that left eight dead. But I'm making the argument that it was a hostage rescue operation, not a criminal assault. We'll see," Walsh said.

"And me? Am I under arrest?"

"No. You're a material witness and a person of interest, but not a suspect. You'll stay in protective custody for now—both for your safety and ours. After that..." Walsh shrugged. "Depends on how the investigation goes."

They took Atlas to a safe house—a nondescript apartment in a residential neighborhood. His family was already there, looking exhausted but relieved to see him.

"Daddy!" Emma and Josh ran to him.

Atlas scooped them up, held them close. For the

first time in three days, they were all together and relatively safe.

That night, after the kids were asleep, Atlas sat with his mother and Sarah in the living room of the safe house. The TV was on, showing news coverage of the Project Genesis scandal.

A news anchor reported: "FBI raids biotech facilities in three states, over seventy arrested..."

Another said: "Edmund Carver officially named as suspect, whereabouts unknown..."

A third announced: "Dr. Lawrence Ashford apprehended at airport attempting to flee country..."

A reporter added: "Families of victims begin coming forward, demanding answers..."

It was everywhere. The story had consumed the news cycle completely. Project Genesis, the experiments, the deaths—all of it exposed for the world to see.

"Your father did this," his mother said softly. "He started all of this with his investigation."

"We finished it," Atlas replied. "Dad started it, Morrison continued it, and we finished it."

"Do you think it's really over?" his mother asked.

Atlas thought about what Hollis had said. About the other investors, the possibility of Project Genesis continuing under a different name.

"No. Not yet. But it will be," he said.

His phone buzzed. Atlas checked it—a text from Hollis: "Saw the news about Ashford's arrest. We're winning, Atlas. How are you holding up?"

Atlas typed back: "I'm okay. Family's safe. That's what matters."

Hollis replied: "The FBI contacted me. Want me to come in for questioning too. I'm going to cooperate, give them everything I have."

Atlas texted: "Good. The more evidence they have, the stronger the cases."

Hollis wrote: "Atlas... when this is all over, when the trials are done and we can breathe again... I'd like to see you. For real, not just as partners in an investigation."

Atlas looked at his ex-wife, at his children sleeping in the other room, at the life he was trying to rebuild from the wreckage.

He typed: "I'd like that too. But I need to focus on my family right now. They need me."

Hollis responded: "I understand. Take care of them. And Atlas? You did good. Better than good. You're a hero."

Atlas texted back: "I don't feel like a hero. I feel like someone who did terrible things for good reasons."

Hollis replied: "That's what heroes are. People who do hard things when no one else will. Sleep well, Atlas. You've earned it."

Atlas set down his phone and looked out the window at the quiet suburban street. Somewhere out there, Edmund Carver was hiding, planning his next move. Somewhere, other billionaires connected to Project Genesis were scrambling to cover their tracks.

The fight wasn't over. Not by a long shot.

But tonight, his family was safe. The truth was public. Justice was beginning. It was a start.

Chapter 8: Hunting Carver

Three days later, Atlas sat in another FBI conference room. This one was larger, with a long table and screens showing maps, photographs, and data feeds. Director Walsh stood at the head of the table, Assistant Director Moss beside him. Six other federal agents filled the remaining seats.

"Thank you all for coming," Walsh said. "Mr. Drummond, this is the task force assigned to locate Edmund Carver. They've been briefed on everything you've provided so far. Today, we need your help narrowing down where he might have gone."

Atlas looked at the screens. One showed a map of the United States with dozens of red dots. Another displayed surveillance footage from various locations. A third listed known associates of Edmund Carver.

"That's a lot of red dots," Atlas observed.

"Properties owned by Carver or his shell companies," Moss explained. "We've checked most of them. He's not there. Either he's moved on, or he's somewhere we haven't identified yet."

"What about his cancer treatments?" Atlas asked.

"He's dying. Stage four pancreatic cancer. He can't just disappear—he needs medical care."

Walsh nodded. "Good point. We've been monitoring oncology centers, but nothing so far. He might have arranged for private care."

"Or he's given up on treatment," one of the other agents suggested. "Decided to die on his own terms rather than in prison."

"I don't think so," Atlas said. "Carver funded Project Genesis specifically to find a cure for himself. He's not the type to give up. He'll keep fighting until the end."

"Which means he needs access to experimental treatments," Moss said. "Treatments that might not be available through legitimate channels."

"Exactly," Atlas agreed. "Which brings us back to Project Genesis. Are all the facilities shut down?"

"The three main ones, yes. Nevada, Georgia, and New York—all raided, all personnel arrested,"

Walsh confirmed. "But your father's files mentioned six facilities total. We're still trying to locate the other three."

Atlas thought about the evidence his father had compiled. "The other three were outside the US. One in Mexico, two in South America. Dad couldn't pin down exact locations, but he had narrowed it to general regions."

"Mexico and South America are big places," one of the agents said. "We can't just raid entire countries looking for secret research facilities."

"No, but you can follow the money," Atlas suggested. "Carver had to fund these facilities. There will be financial transactions, wire transfers, shell companies funneling money south of the border. Find the money trail, you find the facilities."

Moss pulled up a new screen showing financial data. "We've been working on that. Your father documented dozens of transactions, but they're layered through so many shell companies it's hard to track. We need someone with expertise in forensic accounting to untangle it."

"What about Hollis?" Atlas asked. "She's been working with the evidence longer than anyone. She might be able to help."

"Ms. Brooks has been cooperating fully," Walsh said. "In fact, she's been incredibly helpful. But there's something you should know."

Atlas felt a chill. "What?"

"Two days ago, someone tried to access her apartment. Security cameras caught two men attempting to break in. They fled when the alarm went off, but we got good footage of their faces." Walsh pulled up images on the screen. "These men work for a private military contractor called Aegis Solutions—the same company that employed Victor Kozlov and the other guards at the exchange site."

"They're still coming after us," Atlas said. "Even with everything public, even with the arrests."

"Not everyone involved in Project Genesis has been caught yet," Moss explained. "There are loose ends. People who have a lot to lose if more evidence comes to light. People who might want to eliminate witnesses."

"Is Hollis safe?" Atlas demanded.

"She's in protective custody, similar to your family," Walsh assured him. "But this confirms what we suspected—there are still active threats out there. Which is why we need to move quickly on Carver and the remaining facilities."

Atlas's phone buzzed. He checked it—a text from Hollis: "Are you in the task force meeting? Walsh mentioned he was briefing you."

Atlas glanced at Walsh, who nodded permission. Atlas typed back: "Yeah. They told me about the break-in attempt. Are you okay?"

Hollis replied: "I'm fine. FBI has me locked down tight. But Atlas, I found something in the financial records. Something big. We need to talk. In person."

Atlas showed the message to Walsh. "Hollis says she found something important. Can we bring her in?"

Walsh considered this. "Let me make a call."

Thirty minutes later, Hollis arrived at the federal building. She was escorted by two agents and looked tired but determined. When she saw

Atlas, her face lit up briefly before returning to professional mode.

"Thanks for coming, Ms. Brooks," Walsh said. "You mentioned you found something significant?"

"Yes." Hollis pulled out her laptop and connected it to the conference room's display system. "I've been analyzing the shell company structures that Carver used to fund Project Genesis. Most of them are dead ends—layers of corporations that ultimately loop back to nothing. But I found an anomaly."

She pulled up a complex diagram showing connections between various companies. "This shell company here—GeneTech Holdings Limited, registered in the Cayman Islands—received significant funding from Helix Innovations. But unlike the others, it didn't just disappear into a black hole. It made regular payments to a facility in Paraguay."

"Paraguay?" Walsh leaned forward. "That's new. We haven't seen Paraguay come up before."

"That's because Atlas's father's investigation didn't get this far," Hollis explained. "But Morrison's files included some additional financial data that filled in the gaps. This facility in Paraguay has been operating for at least five years. It's one of the original Project Genesis sites."

"Do we have a location?" Moss asked.

"City called Encarnación, on the border with Argentina," Hollis confirmed. "The facility is registered as a pharmaceutical research lab, totally legitimate on paper. But the timing and amounts of the payments match exactly with the pattern used for the other illegal facilities."

"That's where he is," Atlas said suddenly. "That's where Carver went."

"What makes you so sure?" Walsh asked.

"Think about it. He's wounded, on the run, needs medical care that no legitimate hospital will provide. The US facilities are all shut down, but if there's still one operating in Paraguay, that's where he'd go. It's remote enough that the FBI can't just roll in, it's got the equipment and personnel he needs, and it's outside US jurisdiction."

Walsh nodded slowly. "That makes sense. We need to verify this facility exists and that Carver is actually there. Give us twenty-four hours to gather intelligence—satellite imagery, security assessments, confirmation of activity."

"Can we afford to wait twenty-four hours?" Atlas asked.

"We can't afford not to," Walsh replied. "If we move on bad intelligence and Carver isn't there, we've blown our chance and he'll disappear completely. We do this right, which means we do it methodically."

Atlas wanted to argue, but Walsh was right. Better to wait a day and be certain than to rush in blind.

"Fine. Twenty-four hours," Atlas agreed. "But after that, we move."

"Agreed," Walsh said. "In the meantime, both of

you stay in protective custody. No unnecessary risks."

After the meeting, Atlas and Hollis were escorted to a secure room where they could wait. As soon as the door closed behind the agents, Hollis turned to him.

"Are you sure about this?" she asked. "About going to Paraguay if Walsh confirms Carver is there?"

"Completely sure. Carver can't be allowed to escape. And I'm not waiting months for international legal processes to play out."

"Then I'm coming with you," Hollis said firmly.

"Hollis—"

"Don't. We've been through this before. I'm part of this investigation. I know the evidence better than anyone except you. And besides, you'll need someone who can handle the digital side—accessing the facility's computers, copying their research data, making sure nothing gets destroyed."

"It's going to be dangerous. More dangerous than the exchange."

"I know. But I'm done hiding while other people fight." Hollis met his eyes. "My father was murdered by these people. I deserve to be there when we take them down."

Atlas studied her face, saw the determination there. He knew that look—he'd seen it in his own mirror enough times.

"Okay," he said. "But you follow my lead. You stay close to me at all times. And you do exactly what I say, when I say it. Agreed?"

"Agreed."

They spent the rest of the day in the safe room, reviewing the financial data Hollis had compiled, planning contingencies. Atlas made calls to Rodriguez and his team, warning them they might have work soon. Everyone confirmed they were ready to move on short notice.

That evening, Hollis's phone alarm went off. "Check-in time," she said.

Atlas watched as she pulled up her laptop and logged into the encrypted system that controlled her dead-man switches. She entered passwords, verified her identity, confirmed her status.

The screen updated: Next check-in required: 3:00 AM, Thursday, October 30th.

"Done," Hollis said. "If I miss that check-in, everything releases automatically. The additional evidence, the connections to the other investors, all of it goes public."

"You're still maintaining the switches?" Atlas asked.

"Of course. The evidence is our insurance policy. As long as it exists and they can't get to it, they can't afford to kill us." Hollis smiled grimly. "It's the same principle as before. Except now, we're using it to hunt them instead of hiding from them."

"And you're certain the release protocols are secure? That no one can intercept or block them?"

"Completely certain. I've distributed the evidence across multiple platforms, multiple countries, multiple redundant systems. If I miss a check-in, everything goes public within minutes. Not even the FBI could stop it." Hollis paused. "Which is why Walsh is being so cooperative. He knows that if anything happens to us, his investigation gets a massive information dump whether he wants it or not."

"Smart," Atlas admitted.

"I learned from the best." Hollis looked at him seriously. "Your father spent months building that evidence. He died protecting it. I'm not going to let it be wasted."

The next morning, Atlas was back in the FBI conference room. This time, Walsh had news.

"We've confirmed the Paraguay facility is still operating," Walsh announced, pulling up satellite imagery on the screens. "These images were taken twelve hours ago. You can see people coming and going, vehicles in the parking area, lights on in multiple buildings."

"So it's active," Atlas said.

"Very active. There's also a private airstrip nearby." Walsh pulled up more images. "And we tracked a flight from Mexico City that landed there three days ago. The flight was chartered by one of Carver's shell companies."

"That's him," Atlas confirmed.

"Most likely," Walsh agreed. He pulled up detailed images of the facility. "The compound is more fortified than we expected. High walls, security cameras, at least a dozen guards based on what we can see from satellite. It's not going to be an easy extraction."

"It never is," Atlas replied.

"There's something else." Moss opened a new file on the screen. "While we were investigating the Paraguay facility, we identified at least two of the other billionaire investors Hollis mentioned. One is Richard Keating, founder of BioLogic Pharmaceuticals. The other is Patricia Delacroix, venture capitalist specializing in biotech investments. Both have connections to Helix Innovations and both have made significant unexplained payments to offshore accounts."

"So you've confirmed what Hollis suspected. She mentioned Morrison had identified other investors but didn't have solid proof," Atlas said.

"Not even close. We think there might be as many as five or six major investors who funded Project Genesis collectively. They shared the costs and the potential benefits." Walsh's expression was grim. "Which means even with Carver captured, the others might try to continue the operation somewhere else."

"Not if we expose all of them," Hollis interjected. "I've been working on tracking the financial connections. Give me another week with Morrison's files and the data from the raids, and I can identify all the investors."

"Will we have a week?" Atlas asked. "Once we grab Carver, the others will know we're coming for them.

They'll destroy evidence, flee the country, hide assets."

"Which is why we need to move on all of them simultaneously," Walsh said. "Get Carver from Paraguay, execute warrants on Keating and Delacroix in the US, and raid whatever other facilities we can locate. Hit them all at once so none of them can warn the others."

"That's a lot of coordination," Moss observed.

"But it's the only way to make sure we get them all." Walsh looked at Atlas. "Now, I need to be very clear about something. Officially, the FBI cannot and will not authorize any illegal operation in Paraguay. We cannot provide material support, intelligence assistance, or any resources that would implicate us in a violation of international law."

"But unofficially?" Atlas asked.

"Unofficially, if a private citizen with knowledge of Edmund Carver's location were to organize an operation to extract an American fugitive from a foreign country, and if that operation were to successfully bring said fugitive back to US soil where he could face justice..." Walsh smiled slightly. "Well, we'd be very grateful. And we might be inclined to view that private citizen's previous actions in an even more favorable light."

"So you're giving me a green light," Atlas said.

"I'm telling you that if you choose to act on your own initiative, we won't stop you. And if you succeed, there might be certain legal benefits." Walsh's expression turned serious. "But understand this—if you go to Paraguay and things go wrong, you're on your own. We can't extract you. We can't protect you diplomatically. You'll be in a foreign country, operating without authorization, with no backup."

"I understand," Atlas said.

"You'll need weapons, equipment, transportation," Moss added. "We obviously can't provide those things officially."

"I have contacts," Atlas said. "People who can help with logistics."

"Of course you do." Walsh pulled out a folder and slid it across the table. "This contains copies of the satellite imagery and our security assessment of the facility. Purely informational, you understand. Not operational support."

Atlas took the folder. "Understood."

"How soon can you be ready?" Walsh asked.

"Forty-eight hours. I need to brief my team, arrange for equipment, and plan the operation."

"Make it happen." Walsh stood up. "And Mr. Drummond? Bring that bastard home."

"One more thing," Atlas said before leaving. "When I bring Carver back, I want my team's immunity guaranteed. In writing. No exceptions, no loopholes."

Walsh nodded. "Done. You bring me Carver, I'll make sure your people walk free."

After the meeting, Atlas and Hollis were escorted back to their respective safe houses. But before they parted, Atlas stopped her in the hallway.

"Are you absolutely sure about coming to Paraguay?" he asked quietly. "It's not going to be a controlled operation. It's going to be messy, improvised, dangerous."

"I'm sure," Hollis said. "But I also know that my dead-man switch is still active. If something happens to me in Paraguay, if I miss my 3 AM check-in, all the additional evidence releases automatically—including the connections to the other billionaire investors that we've been holding back."

"So even if things go wrong, the truth still gets out," Atlas said.

"Exactly. It's our insurance policy." Hollis smiled. "And it's leverage. Walsh knows that if anything happens to us, his investigation gets flooded with evidence whether he wants it or not. That's why he's being so cooperative."

Atlas spent the evening making calls. Rodriguez answered on the first ring.

"Tell me you've got work," Rodriguez said without preamble.

"How do you feel about Paraguay?" Atlas asked.

"Never been. Is it nice this time of year?"

"Probably not where we're going." Atlas filled him in on the situation—Carver's location, the facility, the unofficial FBI approval. "I need four good men. Ones who aren't afraid of international complications."

"I can have that for you in twenty-four hours," Rodriguez confirmed. "Same team as before?"

"If they're willing. This is purely voluntary. No one's obligated."

"Ace, you saved my life in Kandahar. You gave me a job when I got out and had nothing. I'd follow you into hell if you asked." Rodriguez paused. "Besides, these Project Genesis assholes tried to kill you and your family. That makes it personal for all of us."

After hanging up with Rodriguez, Atlas called Marcus, then Davis, then Torres. All of them said yes without hesitation. Rodriguez also brought in two additional contractors—Cooper and Vega—men Atlas didn't know personally but who came with Rodriguez's strong recommendation.

Within two hours, Atlas had his team confirmed.

"The FBI released Atlas and Hollis from protective custody the morning of the departure. Walsh made it clear: they were on their own now. No official support, no backup, no protection if things went wrong. Exactly as promised."

Two days later, Atlas stood on the tarmac of a private airfield outside Houston. A chartered cargo plane waited, its engines idling. Rodriguez, Marcus, Davis, Torres, Cooper, and Vega were loading equipment—weapons, body armor, communications gear, medical supplies.

Hollis stood beside Atlas, wearing tactical clothing and looking determined despite obvious nervousness.

"Last chance to back out," Atlas told her.

"I'm not backing out," Hollis replied. "I've come this far. I'm seeing it through."

"You know the plan?"

"Stay with you at all times. Don't try to be a hero. Once we confirm Carver's location, I access their computer systems and copy everything while your team secures the facility. Then we extract and get out."

"And if things go wrong?"

"Then I improvise and try not to get killed." Hollis smiled slightly. "Just like everyone else."

Rodriguez approached. "We're loaded and ready. Flight time to Paraguay is approximately nine hours. I've arranged for ground transportation and a safe house once we land. After that, we've got twenty-four hours before people start asking questions."

"Then we don't waste any time," Atlas said. "We land, we gear up, we hit the facility, and we're out within twelve hours."

"Fast and dirty," Rodriguez agreed. "My favorite kind of operation."

They boarded the plane. As it taxied down the

runway, Atlas looked out the window at the receding lights of Houston. Somewhere in that city, his children were sleeping in a safe house, protected by federal agents. His mother and ex-wife were with them.

He was leaving them again. Going into danger again. But this time, it was to finish what his father had started. To ensure that the people responsible for Project Genesis faced justice.

The plane lifted off, climbing into the night sky. Atlas closed his eyes and tried to rest. Tomorrow would bring another fight, another risk of death.

But at least this time, they were hunting instead of being hunted.

And Atlas Drummond was very good at hunting.

Chapter 9: The Paraguay Extraction

The plane landed at a private airfield outside Asunción, not the main commercial airport. No customs, no inspections—just a small landing strip used by wealthy landowners and businessmen who valued privacy. They taxied to a remote hangar where Rodriguez's contact had arranged for two SUVs to be waiting.

Atlas had slept fitfully during the nine-hour flight, his mind running through contingencies and backup plans. Now, as they unloaded their equipment in the predawn darkness, he felt the familiar pre-mission clarity settling over him.

"Three-hour drive to Encarnación," Rodriguez said, checking a map on his phone. "We'll stop at the safe house first, do final equipment checks, then move on the facility after dark."

"Good," Atlas agreed. "We hit them at midnight. They'll have skeleton crew security, hopefully most of the scientists will be sleeping."

They drove south through Paraguay's countryside, watching the landscape change from urban sprawl to rural farmland to rolling hills. The roads were decent but not great—two lanes of cracked asphalt with occasional

potholes.

Hollis sat beside Atlas in the second vehicle, her laptop open, reviewing the facility schematics Walsh had provided.

"According to the satellite imagery, there are three main buildings," she said. "The largest one in the center is probably where they do the actual research. The two smaller buildings on either side are likely housing for staff and security."

"How many people total?" Atlas asked.

"Hard to say for certain. Based on the size and the vehicles we can see in the parking area, maybe forty to fifty people. But we don't know how many are security versus scientists versus support staff."

"We have to assume at least a dozen armed guards," Davis said from the driver's seat. "Probably more if Carver is really there. He'll want protection."

"Which is why we go in fast and hard," Atlas said. "Overwhelming force, quick extraction. We're not there to fight—we're there to grab Carver and get out."

They reached the safe house—a small farmhouse on the outskirts of Encarnación—just before noon. Rodriguez had rented it through an intermediary, paying

cash for a month with no questions asked.

The team unloaded their equipment and began final preparations. Weapons were cleaned and checked. Body armor was fitted. Communications equipment was tested. Rodriguez set up a portable satellite internet terminal on the roof—essential equipment for operations in remote areas. Everyone reviewed the plan one more time.

"We go in two teams," Atlas explained, using a hand-drawn map of the facility. "Rodriguez, you take Marcus and Vega. You're team one—primary assault. You breach the main gate, create chaos, draw their security to the front of the compound."

Rodriguez nodded, marking positions on the map.

"Davis, you're overwatch. Find high ground with a good view of the compound. You provide cover fire if things go bad," Atlas continued.

"Roger that," Davis confirmed.

"Torres and Cooper, you fall back early and position our vehicles at two different rally points for extraction. We'll need immediate pickup when we come out."

Both men nodded.

"Hollis and I are team two. While Rodriguez's team has their attention, we breach from the side, go for the computer systems and Carver. We copy everything on their servers, grab Carver, and extract."

"What if Carver isn't in the main building?" Vega asked.

"Then we adapt. But according to Walsh's assessment, the main building has medical facilities. That's where a dying man would be receiving treatment." Atlas looked around the room. "Questions?"

"What if the Paraguayan police show up?" Marcus asked.

"We avoid engagement if possible. But we're not leaving without Carver." Atlas's voice was hard. "This is our one shot. We don't get a second chance."

They spent the afternoon resting and making final preparations. Atlas tried to sleep but couldn't. His mind kept going over the plan, looking for flaws, trying to anticipate what could go wrong.

At 6 PM, Hollis's phone alarm went off.

"Check-in time," she said quietly.

Atlas watched as she connected her laptop to Rodriguez's satellite internet terminal. The connection was slow but stable. She logged into the encrypted system, entered her passwords, completed the verification process.

The screen updated: Next check-in required: 6:00 AM, Friday, October 31st.

"Done," Hollis said. "We've got twelve hours. If we're not out of Paraguay by then..."

"We'll be out," Atlas assured her. "The operation shouldn't take more than two hours. We'll be back at the airport and wheels up long before your next check-in."

"And if something goes wrong? If we get captured or killed?"

"Then the evidence releases automatically. The other investors get exposed. Carver's entire network gets shut down." Atlas took her hand. "Either way, we win."

As darkness fell, the team geared up. Black tactical clothing, body armor, weapons, night vision goggles. They looked like a special operations team —which, in a way, they were.

At 10 PM, they loaded into the vehicles and headed toward the facility.

The drive took forty minutes. They parked the vehicles half a mile away from the compound, hidden in a grove of trees off the main road.

Atlas activated his radio. "Comms check. Everyone sound off."

One by one, the team confirmed their radios were working.

"Davis, move to your overwatch position. You've got thirty minutes," Atlas ordered.

"Roger. Moving now," Davis replied, disappearing into the darkness with his sniper rifle.

"Torres, Cooper—fall back now and get the vehicles positioned," Atlas continued. "Torres, you take rally point alpha on the east side. Cooper, rally point bravo on the south. We'll signal which extraction point we're using when we come out."

"Roger," both men acknowledged, heading back toward the SUVs.

The remaining team waited, checking weapons, adjusting gear, mentally preparing for what was coming.

At 11:45 PM, Davis's voice came over the radio. "Overwatch in position. I have visual on the compound. Counting twelve guards visible, probably more inside. Main building has lights on in the east wing, that's likely where they're working. West wing is dark."

"Copy that," Atlas acknowledged. "Torres, Cooper, status?"

"Rally point alpha, in position," Torres reported.

"Rally point bravo, ready," Cooper confirmed.

"All assault teams, move to breach positions," Atlas ordered.

Rodriguez, Marcus, and Vega moved toward the main gate. Atlas and Hollis circled around to the south side of the compound, approaching a section of perimeter fence that satellite imagery had shown was poorly lit.

At exactly midnight, they were in position.

"Team one, ready," Rodriguez whispered over the radio.

"Team two, ready," Atlas confirmed.

"Overwatch ready," Davis added.

Atlas took a deep breath. This was it.

"Execute," he said quietly.

Rodriguez's team hit the main gate with explosive charges—enough to blow the lock and create chaos. The explosion echoed across the compound, immediately triggering alarms and floodlights.

Guards came running from multiple directions, converging on the front gate and shouting in Spanish. Rodriguez's team engaged them with suppressing fire, driving them back toward cover.

"Go, go, go!" Atlas whispered urgently to Hollis.

While all attention was focused on the front gate assault, Atlas used bolt cutters on the chain-link fence on the south side. He cut a man-sized opening and they slipped through, sprinting toward the main building's side entrance.

Guards ran past them in the darkness, all heading toward the firefight at the front gate. No one saw Atlas and Hollis approaching from the opposite direction.

Atlas reached the side door and placed a small breaching charge on the lock. They stepped back, he triggered it, and the door blew inward.

They were inside.

The interior was sterile, clinical—white walls, fluorescent lighting, the smell of disinfectant. They were

in a corridor with doors on both sides.

"Find the server room," Atlas said. "I'm going for Carver. Stay on comms."

"Atlas, be careful," Hollis said.

"Always am."

They split up. Hollis went left, toward what looked like an IT infrastructure room. Atlas went right, deeper into the building.

He moved quickly but carefully, checking corners, watching for threats. The building seemed mostly empty—the guards were all outside dealing with Rodriguez's assault.

Atlas heard voices ahead—panicked, speaking English. He slowed, crept closer.

A door was open, light spilling out. Inside, Atlas could see medical equipment, monitors, an IV stand. And lying in a hospital bed, looking gaunt and pale, was Edmund Carver.

Two men in white coats stood beside him—doctors or scientists, not security. They were arguing about whether to evacuate him.

Atlas stepped into the doorway, his rifle raised.

"Nobody move," he said in English.

The two men froze, hands going up. Carver turned his head slowly, his eyes focusing on Atlas with effort.

"Mr. Drummond," Carver said, his voice weak but still carrying that cultured accent. "I wondered if you'd find me."

"Get up," Atlas ordered. "You're coming with me."

"I'm afraid that's not possible. As you can see, I'm somewhat... indisposed." Carver gestured weakly at the IV lines and monitors. "I'm dying, Mr. Drummond. The treatments aren't working. I have perhaps two weeks left."

"Then you can die in an American prison instead of a Paraguayan lab. Get up."

"Such determination. Such righteousness." Carver smiled slightly. "You remind me of your father. He had that same stubborn refusal to accept reality."

"Don't talk about my father."

"Why not? I respected Thomas Drummond. He was intelligent, thorough, relentless. If he'd been willing to work with me instead of against me, we could have accomplished great things together."

Atlas moved closer, keeping his rifle trained on Carver. "You killed him."

"I did. And I'd do it again." Carver's smile faded. "Your father was going to destroy everything I'd built. Decades of research, billions of dollars invested, the potential to cure diseases that have plagued humanity for centuries. All of it, gone, because one man decided to play hero."

"You weren't curing diseases. You were murdering people."

"Sacrifices. Necessary sacrifices in pursuit of a greater good." Carver coughed, a wet rattling sound. "Do you know how many people die of cancer every year, Mr. Drummond? Millions. And we were so close to a cure. So close. But your father didn't care about that. He only cared about his narrow definition of morality."

"Those people didn't volunteer to be guinea pigs. You experimented on them without consent. You murdered them."

"I gave them purpose. Most of them were nobody—homeless, addicted, forgotten by society. I gave their deaths meaning."

Atlas felt rage building in his chest. "My father's

death gave his life meaning. Not you."

Gunfire erupted from somewhere in the building. Rodriguez's voice came over the radio: "Guards are pushing into the building from multiple entrances. Heavy resistance. We're falling back to rally point alpha."

"Copy that," Atlas replied. He turned to the two scientists. "Disconnect him from those machines. Now."

They hesitated. Atlas fired a single shot into the ceiling. Both men jumped and immediately began disconnecting Carver's IV lines and monitors.

"You're making a mistake," Carver said as they worked. "Even if you take me back to the US, even if I'm convicted and imprisoned, it won't matter. Project Genesis is bigger than me. There are others who will continue the work. You've won a battle, Mr. Drummond, but you haven't won the war."

"We'll see about that," Atlas said.

His radio crackled. Hollis's voice: "I've got the data. All of it. Downloading to portable drives now, should be done in ninety seconds."

"Make it sixty. This place is getting hot."

The scientists finished disconnecting Carver. Atlas

grabbed the dying man by the arm and hauled him out of bed. Carver's legs buckled—he couldn't stand on his own.

"He can't walk," one of the scientists protested. "He's too weak."

"Then you're going to help me carry him," Atlas ordered, gesturing with his rifle.

Reluctantly, the two scientists supported Carver between them. Atlas kept his weapon ready and started moving toward the exit.

The hallway was chaos now—more guards had entered the building, shots were being fired in multiple directions. Atlas reached an intersection and came face to face with a guard raising an assault rifle. Both men fired simultaneously. The guard went down. Atlas felt something punch into his body armor—painful but not penetrating.

He kept moving, forcing the scientists to drag Carver with them.

Rodriguez's voice on the radio: "Team one is at rally point alpha. Where are you?"

"Thirty seconds out with the package," Atlas replied. "Hollis, status?"

"Done! Data secured, heading for rally point alpha now!"

Atlas fought through two more encounters with guards, his ammunition running low. He reached the fence opening they'd cut earlier and dragged Carver through it. The scientists stumbled after them.

Rally point alpha was two hundred yards away through rough terrain. Atlas could see Torres's SUV, headlights off, engine running.

"Move, move!" Atlas shouted at the scientists.

They half-carried, half-dragged Carver across the uneven ground. Bullets kicked up dirt around them as guards from the compound opened fire.

Davis's rifle cracked from his overwatch position, and several guards went down. "I've got you covered! Keep moving!"

They reached the SUV. Rodriguez, Marcus, and Vega were already there, laying down suppressing fire. Hollis arrived seconds later, clutching her laptop and portable hard drives.

"Load him up!" Atlas ordered.

They threw Carver into the back seat. The two

scientists tried to run back toward the facility, but Marcus grabbed one of them.

"You're coming with us," Marcus said. "We might need a doctor."

The scientist looked terrified but climbed into the vehicle.

"Everyone in! Go, go, go!" Atlas shouted.

Torres floored the accelerator and they roared away from the compound, bouncing over rough ground until they reached the road.

"Cooper, rally point bravo is compromised," Rodriguez said into the radio. "Multiple vehicles heading your direction. Abort and return to the airport."

"Roger, heading to airport now," Cooper confirmed.

Davis's voice: "I'm clear of my position. Moving to my extraction vehicle. See you at the airfield."

The drive back to the airport was tense. Every set of headlights behind them could be pursuit.

Every police car they passed could be responding to reports of the assault.

But their luck held. They reached the private airfield at 3:45 AM without incident.

The cargo plane was waiting, engines already running. Cooper and Davis were already there, having taken different routes. They loaded Carver—barely conscious now—aboard and strapped him down. The team followed, everyone exhausted and bleeding from minor wounds.

The one scientist they'd brought sat in a corner, looking shell-shocked.

As the plane taxied down the runway, Atlas finally allowed himself to breathe. They'd actually pulled it off.

Hollis sat beside him, her laptop and portable drives still clutched in her arms like precious artifacts.

"We did it," she said, disbelief in her voice. "We actually did it."

"Yeah. We did." Atlas looked at Carver, strapped to a seat at the back of the plane, looking small and pathetic. Not a powerful billionaire anymore. Just a dying old man.

"What happens now?" Hollis asked.

"Now we deliver him to Walsh. Let the FBI finish what we started." Atlas checked his watch. 4:15 AM. "You'll be able to do your check-in once we're at altitude

and you can connect to the satellite system."

"Right." Hollis looked relieved. "Can't have the dead-man switch triggering now that we've actually won."

Thirty minutes later, at cruising altitude, Hollis connected to the plane's satellite internet and completed her check-in.

While she was logged in, a new email arrived —from an address Atlas didn't recognize.

The subject line read: "You Got Carver. Now Let's Talk About the Others."

Atlas opened it.

"Mr. Drummond and Ms. Brooks,

Congratulations on your successful operation. Edmund Carver was indeed one of the investors in Project Genesis. But as you've suspected, he wasn't alone.

I represent a coalition of individuals who funded the project. We would like to offer you a business proposition. In exchange for your silence about our involvement, we're prepared to offer you $50 million. Each.

Before you refuse, consider this: Edmund Carver is dying. He'll be dead within weeks regardless of whether he stands trial. But the rest of us have decades of life left. We have resources, connections, power that you can't imagine. We can make your lives very comfortable, or very difficult.

You have 24 hours to decide. Reply to this email with your answer. Choose wisely.

A Friend"

Atlas and Hollis looked at each other.

"They're trying to buy us off," Hollis said.

"Fifty million each," Atlas replied. "That's a lot of money."

"Are you actually considering it?"

"No. But we should string them along. Reply and say we're interested but need proof they can actually pay. Get them to reveal more about who they are."

"While we're preparing to release all the evidence anyway," Hollis finished, understanding.

"Exactly."

Hollis composed a reply: "We're listening. But we'll need verification of funds and identities of all parties involved before we agree to anything. We're not interested in dealing with intermediaries. 24 hours to provide proof."

She hit send.

"Now what?" she asked.

"Now we wait and see how desperate they are," Atlas said. "Desperate people make mistakes. And when they do, we'll be ready."

The plane climbed higher, carrying them away from Paraguay, away from the firefight, toward home and justice.

Edmund Carver was captured. The facility's data was secured. But the fight wasn't over.

The other investors were still out there. Still rich, still powerful, still dangerous.

But now they were scared. And scared people were easier to catch.

Atlas Drummond was going to make sure every single one of them faced justice.

For his father. For Hollis's father. For all the victims of Project Genesis.

This ends when they're all in prison, Atlas thought.

Not before.

Epilogue: Six Months Later

Atlas stood in the courtroom, watching as the judge read the verdict.

"On the charge of conspiracy to commit murder, we find the defendant, Edmund Carver, guilty. On the charge of human experimentation without consent, guilty. On all two hundred and thirty-seven counts of murder, guilty."

The courtroom erupted. Families of victims cried, some in relief, some in anger that it had taken so long. Media reporters typed frantically on their phones and laptops. Federal prosecutors shook hands, congratulating each other.

Edmund Carver sat at the defense table, looking even more skeletal than he had six months ago. The cancer was winning. He'd likely be dead before serving a year of his life sentence.

But he would die in prison. That was what mattered.

Atlas felt a hand slip into his. Hollis stood beside him, her expression satisfied.

"One down," she said quietly.

"Four more to go," Atlas replied.

The other investors had been identified over the past six months. Richard Keating, founder of BioLogic Pharmaceuticals. Patricia Delacroix, venture capitalist. Marcus Tang, pharmaceutical executive. And the last one they'd finally tracked down just three weeks ago—Senator Robert Hargrove, who'd used his political connections to protect Project Genesis from federal oversight.

All of them were under indictment. All of them would stand trial.

The mysterious email offering them fifty million dollars had been traced back to Keating. He'd been desperate to buy their silence, had even transferred five million dollars to a test account to prove he could pay.

That transfer had given the FBI everything they needed to tie him directly to Project Genesis's funding.

After the verdict was read, Atlas and Hollis left the courthouse through a side exit, avoiding the media circus out front. They'd been offered interviews by every major news organization—60 Minutes, Dateline, CNN—but had declined them all.

This wasn't about fame. It was about justice.

Director Walsh was waiting for them outside, leaning against an unmarked FBI vehicle.

"Good verdict," Walsh said as they approached.

"Long overdue," Atlas replied.

"I wanted to update you on the other cases. Keating's trial starts next month. Delacroix's attorneys are trying to negotiate a plea deal, but we're not offering anything less than life without parole. Tang is fighting extradition from Singapore, but we'll get him eventually."

"And Hargrove?" Hollis asked.

Walsh's expression darkened. "That's complicated. He's a sitting US Senator with powerful friends. The Justice Department is moving carefully, building an airtight case. But he will be charged. I promise you that."

"We'll believe it when we see it," Atlas said.

"I understand your skepticism. But Hargrove doesn't have the protection he used to. The scandal has destroyed his political career. His own party has abandoned him. He's toxic now." Walsh straightened. "Speaking of which, I have something for you."

He pulled out an envelope and handed it to Atlas.

"What's this?" Atlas asked.

"Official notification from the Justice Department. All charges against you and your team related to the events of October 25th have been dropped. Self-defense, defense of family. You're clear."

Atlas felt something release in his chest. "And Rodriguez? Marcus? Davis? The others?"

"All clear. Full immunity, as promised." Walsh smiled slightly. "You kept your end of the deal. We kept ours."

"What about the Paraguay operation?"

"What operation?" Walsh's smile widened. "Officially, Edmund Carver was apprehended by FBI agents working with Paraguayan authorities. Your name doesn't appear in any official reports."

"So we were never there."

"Exactly."

Hollis spoke up. "And the additional evidence we provided? The financial records showing the complete network of investors and facilities?"

"Critical to our cases. We've shut down all six Project Genesis facilities, arrested over two hundred people, and identified forty-seven additional victims we didn't know about. Your father's work—" Walsh looked at Atlas "—and Agent Morrison's investigation, and your efforts to finish what they started—all of it has saved lives. Probably hundreds of lives that would have been lost if Project Genesis had continued operating."

Atlas thought about his father, about the obsessive way Thomas Drummond had pursued the truth. About how that pursuit had cost him his life.

"Dad would be proud," Atlas said quietly. "He'd be glad it wasn't for nothing."

"He should be proud. You both should be." Walsh extended his hand. "Thank you. For everything."

They shook hands, then Walsh got in his vehicle and drove away.

Atlas and Hollis walked to Atlas's truck—the old one had been totaled in the firefight, so he'd bought a replacement. Similar model, same color. Some things were worth keeping consistent.

"Where to now?" Hollis asked as they got in.

"I'm picking up the kids from Sarah's place. It's my weekend." Atlas started the engine. "Want to come? Emma's been asking about you."

"Really?"

"Really. She thinks you're 'cool' because you're a hacker who helped catch bad guys." Atlas smiled. "Josh just wants to know if you like dinosaurs."

"I can fake enthusiasm for dinosaurs," Hollis said, smiling back.

They drove to Sarah's house—the same house where Atlas had found his family missing six months ago. The memory still sent a chill through him, but it was getting easier. Time didn't heal all wounds, but it helped.

Sarah answered the door with Emma and Josh bouncing excitedly behind her.

"Daddy!" they both shouted, running to hug him.

Atlas scooped them up, one in each arm, feeling their weight and warmth and aliveness. For a moment after the kidnapping, he'd thought he'd never get to do this again.

"Hey, monsters," he said, setting them down. "Ready for the weekend?"

"Are we going to the zoo?" Josh asked hopefully.

"If you want. We can do whatever you guys want."

Emma noticed Hollis standing slightly behind Atlas. "Is Hollis coming with us?"

"If that's okay with you," Hollis said.

"Yes!" Emma grabbed Hollis's hand. "You can help me with my science project. Dad's not good at science."

"Hey, I'm okay at science," Atlas protested.

"You thought plants breathe oxygen," Emma said, rolling her eyes in that way nine-year-olds perfected.

"Well, they do breathe. Just... differently."

Sarah smiled from the doorway. "Have fun. Bring them back Sunday evening?"

"Will do." Atlas paused. "Thanks, Sarah. For everything. For being so understanding about... everything."

"You saved our lives, Atlas. That buys a lot of understanding." Sarah's expression was warm. "Besides, the kids are happy. That's what matters."

They loaded the kids into the truck and drove toward Atlas's apartment. It was a new place— bigger than the old one, with two bedrooms so Emma and Josh could each have their own space when they visited.

"Can we stop for ice cream?" Josh asked.

"Before lunch?" Atlas replied.

"Please?"

Atlas looked at Hollis, who shrugged. "You're the parent. But I wouldn't say no to ice cream."

"Traitor," Atlas said, but he was smiling. "Fine. Ice cream it is."

They stopped at a local ice cream shop. While the kids debated flavors, Hollis and Atlas sat at a small table by the window.

"You're good with them," Hollis observed, watching Atlas help Josh decide between chocolate and mint chip.

"I try. I wasn't around much when they were younger—the job, the divorce, my own issues. But after everything that happened..." Atlas trailed off. "Life's too short to miss the important stuff."

"Are you happy?" Hollis asked. "Really happy, I mean. Not just relieved that it's over."

Atlas thought about it. Six months ago, his life had been in shambles. His father was dead. His family had been kidnapped. He'd killed eight people and conducted an illegal international operation.

Now, his kids were safe. The people responsible for Project Genesis were facing justice. He had a new job—legitimate security consulting, working for himself, choosing his own clients. And he had Hollis.

"Yeah," he said. "I'm happy. Maybe for the first time in years."

"Good." Hollis smiled. "Because I'm happy too. And I was thinking..."

"Dangerous."

"Shut up." She kicked him lightly under the table. "I was thinking maybe I should look for an apartment here. Instead of in Atlanta. If that would be okay with you."

Atlas felt his heart rate pick up slightly. "You want to move here?"

"I want to be where you are. Where this is." She gestured between them. "We've been doing the long-distance thing for six months. It's working, but I miss you when I'm not here."

"I miss you too."

"So? What do you think?"

"I think you should definitely move here," Atlas said. "And I think when you do, we should talk about maybe getting a place together. Eventually. When you're ready."

"When we're ready," Hollis corrected.

"When we're ready," Atlas agreed.

Emma and Josh returned with enormous ice cream cones, dripping chocolate and sprinkles. They sat at the table, talking over each other about school and friends and the upcoming science fair.

Atlas watched them, feeling a contentment he hadn't known was possible. Six months ago, he'd been fighting for survival. Now he was fighting for normalcy—for weekends with his kids, for a relationship with a woman who understood him, for a life that wasn't defined by violence and loss.

His phone buzzed. Text from Rodriguez: "Got another security contract if you're interested. Nothing crazy, just some consulting work. Good money, zero chance of international incidents."

Atlas texted back: "Send me the details. But I'm only taking jobs that don't involve gunfights."

Rodriguez replied: "Where's the fun in that? But yeah, this one's legitimate. You've gone soft, Ace."

"Maybe. Or maybe I just learned what's important."

"Fair enough. Say hi to the kids for me."

Atlas set down his phone and looked around the ice cream shop. At his children enjoying their treats. At Hollis laughing at something Emma said. At the ordinary, beautiful normalcy of a Saturday afternoon.

This was what his father had died for. Not just to expose Project Genesis, not just to get justice for victims. But to protect moments like these. To make sure families could be together, safe, happy.

Thomas Drummond had spent his life pursuing truth and justice. In the end, it had cost him everything.

But it had given Atlas back everything that mattered.

"Dad, you're smiling weird," Josh said, chocolate ice cream smeared across his face.

"Am I?"

"Yeah. Like a weirdo."

"Well, that's because I am a weirdo," Atlas said, reaching over to wipe Josh's face with a napkin.

"A happy weirdo," Emma added.

"Yeah," Atlas agreed, looking at Hollis, who smiled back. "A happy weirdo."

Epilogue: Three Months Later

The final trial concluded on a cold February morning. Senator Robert Hargrove was found guilty on all counts—conspiracy to commit murder, obstruction of justice, misuse of public office, and seventeen counts of accessory to murder.

His sentencing hearing was scheduled for the following month, but legal experts predicted he would receive life in prison without possibility of parole.

All five of Project Genesis's primary investors were now either convicted or awaiting sentencing. The organization had been completely dismantled. Every facility shut down. Every piece of research destroyed or seized as evidence.

It was over.

Atlas watched the news coverage from his new apartment—the one he now shared with Hollis, who'd moved to Houston three months earlier. Her things were everywhere—books stacked on shelves, her computer equipment taking up one corner of the living room, her coffee mug perpetually sitting on the kitchen counter.

It felt like home.

"They're calling you a hero again," Hollis said, reading her phone. "Another article about how you exposed the biggest biotech scandal in history."

"I didn't expose it. Dad did. Morrison did. I just finished what they started."

"Don't sell yourself short. You risked everything—your life, your freedom, your future with your kids. You didn't have to do that."

"Yeah, I did. Some things are worth the risk."

Hollis set down her phone and moved to sit beside him on the couch. "Any regrets?"

Atlas thought about it honestly. "I regret that Dad didn't live to see this. I regret that Morrison didn't get to finish her investigation. I regret the eight people I killed, even though they were trying to kill me."

"But?"

"But I don't regret saving my family. I don't regret stopping Project Genesis. And I don't regret meeting you in that bar six months ago."

"It's been nine months, actually."

"Has it?" Atlas smiled. "Time flies when you're conducting illegal operations in foreign countries."

"And when you're falling in love," Hollis added quietly.

Atlas looked at her. They'd danced around the word for months, both knowing it but not quite saying it out loud.

"Yeah," he agreed. "That too."

They sat in comfortable silence, watching the news coverage wind down. Another case closed. Another chapter finished.

But life went on. Emma had her science fair next week. Josh's birthday was coming up. Atlas had three consulting contracts lined up. Hollis was teaching cybersecurity courses at a local college.

Normal life. Beautiful, ordinary, precious life.

Atlas's phone buzzed. Text from his mother: "Dinner at my place Sunday? I'm making your father's favorite pot roast. Thought we could remember him together."

Atlas typed back: "We'll be there. Can I bring Hollis?"

"Of course. She's family now."

Family. The word hit Atlas harder than he expected. He'd lost his father, but he'd gained so much else. A stronger relationship with his mother. A better relationship with his kids. A partner who understood him completely.

"Everything okay?" Hollis asked, noticing his expression.

"Yeah. Everything's good." Atlas put his arm around her. "Better than good, actually. Everything's right."

They sat together on the couch as the afternoon light faded, two people who'd found each other in the darkest moment of their lives and had somehow built something beautiful from the wreckage.

Thomas Drummond's investigation had exposed evil and brought justice to hundreds of victims.

But more than that, it had brought Atlas and Hollis together. Had given Atlas back his purpose, his direction, his reason to keep fighting.

His father had died pursuing truth.

But in doing so, he'd given Atlas life.

And that, Atlas thought, was the greatest legacy any father could leave.

THE END

A Note To Readers

If you made it this far, thank you.

At 84, publishing this novel feels both impossible and inevitable. Impossible because I should have done this decades ago. Inevitable because this story wouldn't leave me alone until I wrote it.

Atlas Drummond: Fragments of Deceit is fiction, but it's built on truths I learned over forty years of service—about what institutions are capable of when no one's watching, about what ordinary people will do when their families are threatened, and about the uncomfortable reality that sometimes the system designed to protect us fails, and individuals must step into the gap.

If this story resonated with you—if Atlas and Hollis's fight for justice kept you turning pages—I would be deeply grateful if you'd take a moment to leave a review on Amazon or Goodreads.

As an independent author, your reviews are everything. They help other readers find the book.

They tell me what worked and what didn't. And they make this entire journey worthwhile.

Reviews don't need to be long or elaborate. A few honest sentences about what you thought is perfect.

Thank you for giving an 84-year-old debut author a chance. Thank you for spending your time with Atlas Drummond. And thank you for supporting independent fiction.

With sincere gratitude,

Jackie L. Smith

Acknowledgments

This book exists because of people who believed in me even when I wasn't sure I believed in myself.

To my family—you endured forty years of military obligations, hospital emergencies, and Air Force deployments. You sacrificed holidays, birthdays, and countless ordinary moments so I could serve. Now you've been patient with one more obsession: an 84-year-old hunched over a computer, muttering about plot holes and character arcs. Thank you for your grace, your humor, and your unwavering support.

To the sailors I served with in the Navy—you taught me about courage, sacrifice, and what it means to face impossible odds with steady hands and dark humor. Atlas Drummond is fiction, but his determination comes from every service member I had the honor of serving alongside.

To the healthcare professionals I worked with during my hospital administration years—you showed me that fighting for others isn't always dramatic. Sometimes it's paperwork, budgets, and bureaucracy. Sometimes it's choosing to care when the system makes caring difficult.

To my Air Force colleagues during my civilian years—you reminded me that service doesn't end when you take off the uniform. Some of the best patriots I've known never wore a name tag.

To the technology that made this possible—I learned computers late in life, but they opened a door I thought had closed forever. At 84, you can still learn new things. You can still chase dreams. You can still surprise yourself.

And to you, the reader—thank you for taking a chance on a debut author who's older than most thriller writers' grandparents. I hope Atlas's story was worth your time.

If it was, please consider leaving a review. It means more than you know.

About The Author

Jackie L. Smith (that's me) served his country for more than four decades before turning to the thriller genre he's loved his entire life.

After twenty years in the United States Navy, he transitioned to healthcare administration, running a hospital in Oklahoma for eight years. He then spent an additional twenty years as a civilian supporting the United States Air Force, bringing his unique combination of military experience and business expertise—honed through his Master's degree in Business Management—to complex operational challenges.

Now 84, Jackie L. Smith has finally carved out time for the pursuits he's always loved: building his stamp and coin collections, staying current with computer technology, and writing the kind of page-turning thriller that kept him up late during all those years of service.

Atlas Drummond: Fragments of Deceit represents a lifetime of observing how institutions work, how power operates in shadows, and what happens when ordinary people are forced to make extraordinary choices. The authenticity in these pages comes from decades spent navigating the intersection of military operations, healthcare systems, and government bureaucracy.

He's already planning another novel.

He currently resides in Staffordsville, Kentucky.

Connect With The Author

Enjoyed Atlas Drummond: Fragments of Deceit?

Please consider leaving a review on Amazon, Goodreads, or your favorite book platform. Reviews help other readers discover books they might love and support authors—especially debut authors at 84—in continuing to write stories that matter.

Recommend this book to friends who enjoy:

• Military and conspiracy thrillers with authentic detail

• Stories about ordinary people forced into extraordinary circumstances

• Fast-paced action balanced with emotional depth

• Realistic portrayals of institutional corruption and the pursuit of justice

• Father-son legacies and the cost of doing what's right

Stay Connected:

Twitter/X: @CheckerBoa81267

Facebook: jacksmith1591

Thank you for reading Atlas Drummond: Fragments of Deceit. Your support means everything to this author and the books success.

At 84, I've finally found my voice. With your help, I hope to keep telling stories that keep you up at night.

— Jackie L. Smith